A FRAGILE THING

Stephanie Ellis

Also By Stephanie Ellis

<u>**Novels**</u>
The Five Turns of the Wheel
Reborn
The Woodcutter
The Barricade
Harrowfield
Twiggy Voo?
A Fragile Thing

<u>**Novellas**</u>
Rat-She
Paused
Bottled
Mason Gorey: A Haunting Catskill Elegy
(with Shane Douglas Keene)

<u>**Short Story Collections**</u>
Devil Kin
Darklings I and II
The Reckoning
As the Wheel Turns

For Katie, Boy Sam, Girl Sam, and Music Mike

May your strength and resilience shine on

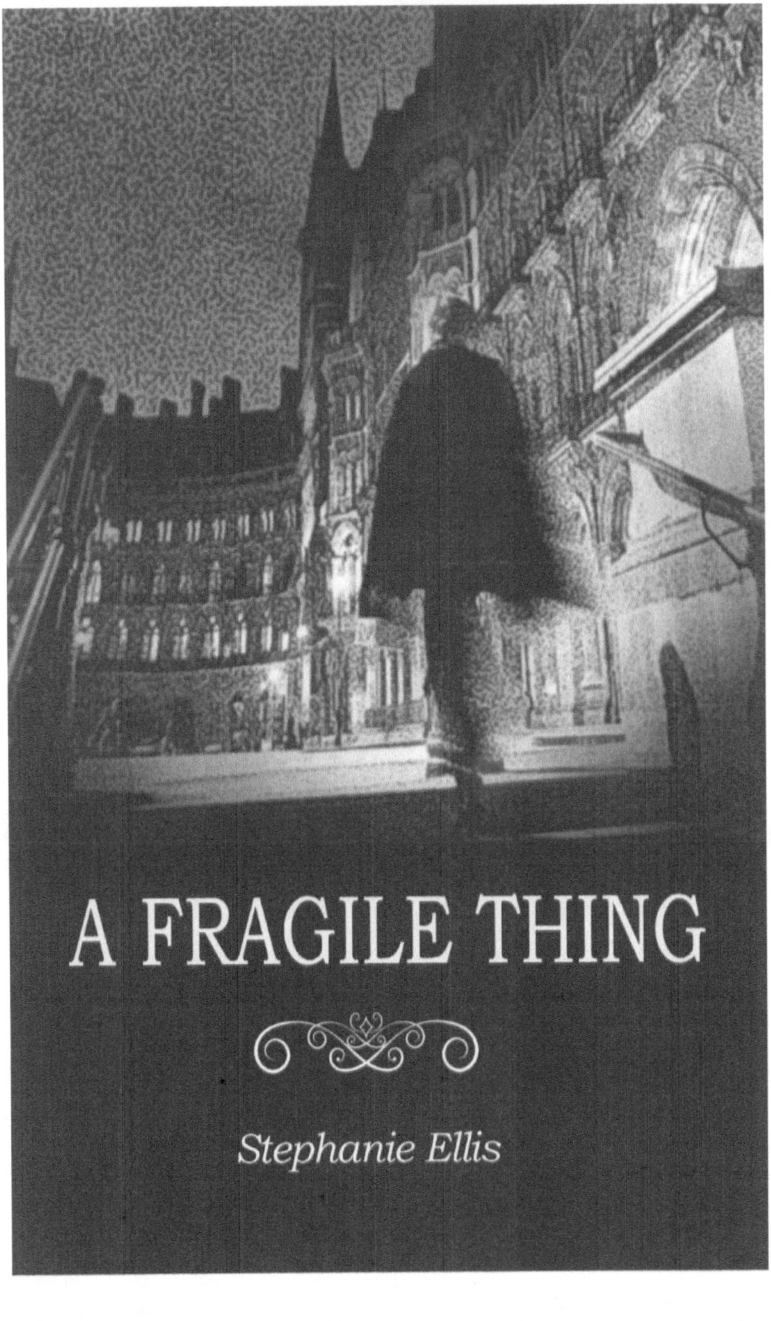

A FRAGILE THING

Stephanie Ellis

Published by Watertower Hill Publishing
Joshua Daughrity - Publisher
www.watertowerhill.com

Cover and internal artwork by Susan Roddey
at The Snark Shop by Pheonix and Fae Creations.

Library of Congress Control Number: XXXXXXXXX

Hardback ISBN: *978-1-965546-27-7*
Paperback ISBN: *978-1-965546-28-4*
eBook ASIN:

Printed in the United States of America
10 9 8 7 6 5 4 3 2 1

Chapter One

Isaac looked once more at the card in his hand. This *was* the address, of that there was no doubt.

He surveyed the dark and deserted streets, noted the occasional shape flit in and out of the shadows. He did not wonder at the business they pursued, only that they left him unmolested. Barely any light reached him as night dressed him in its familiar cloak, a comforting presence keeping him hidden. He disliked the day; it showed him too much, reminded him too much of what he really was.

Above, houses grabbed towards each other in attempted embrace, their rapture keeping out the moon's searching beam. Broken windows and rotting shutters reflected nothing of any life. Doorways hung wide open, empty mouths unbreached, ignored … hungry.

Pools of liquid gathered amongst broken cobbles, their paths sneaking their way between adulterous houses.

Isaac knew this world. It was his birthright, even though he showed another face to society, and now it reached out to reclaim him, as he had always known it would.

He started down the steps. Seven, he calculated from street level, but as he descended there appeared to be more. He lost count. *How could he lose count?*

Down, down. Each step as invisible as the preceding one, each wearing that same cloak of invisibility as himself, each requiring a leap of faith. He tried to keep track again. One, two … seven … eleven. But still they went on.

A wave of vertigo hit him; nausea rising up, threatening to unbalance him. His legs started to tremble, defying his resolve. His arm reached out for the wall in an effort to steady himself.

Nothing. There was nothing there and he felt as if he would fall. Only the promise of wealth and power drew him on. Then a door opened, casting a gentle glow around him. Isaac glanced back up. Seven.

A burly figure appeared, hand out ready for his invitation; Isaac had been warned there'd be no admittance without it. He handed over the card, suffered the appraising look of the man, an evil-looking specimen if ever there was one, and allowed him to close the door on the city behind him.

Isaac found himself in a small room. That was a surprise. Yet this was no gin palace, no penny gaff. Everything about it spoke quality, from the heavy drapes to the crystal lamps and finely carved tables. An oddity in the depths of the Rookeries.

Then he remembered the man who'd issued him the invitation. He'd worn a fine woollen coat, the softest leather gloves, carried an ivory cane. Everything about him spoke quality; a quality Isaac coveted. Life had been getting harder of late and Isaac realised that without help from the right quarters he would soon slip back into the mire from which he had barely escaped. He was prepared to take a shortcut or two to get on.

A waiter guided him to his seat, placed a decanter and glass in front of him. "Enjoy the show, sir."

Isaac was left to his thoughts, puzzling over the riddle of the place. There were others, like him, sat one to a table, each looking at the stage. He could make nothing out beyond a vague idea of their general shape and size, nothing familiar about any of them, except the sense that maybe they were kindred spirits. He could detect no malice, no hint of imminent danger; growing up on the streets had given him a keen survivor's instinct which had served him well in the past. For the moment he would continue to trust to it.

He was snapped out of his trance when the lamps on the wall dimmed. The only light that remained was focussed on the stage. A young girl sat there. Barely more than an urchin, clad in rags, deathly pale. There was something, *someone*, else behind her; a presence without form.

"Lucy," said a voice; crooning, soothing.

Isaac could see the shape of a mouth murmuring into her ear. Saw her turn to listen, nod, and smile.

"Lucy," repeated the voice. "How many souls do we have here tonight?"

"Ten," she replied.

An audience of ten. Not many. How did the man make his money, especially if the others were like himself?

"And who do you see in the shadows?"

"Him," said Lucy. She pointed directly at Isaac.

Isaac started. Felt his pulse begin to race. Her gaze was intense, uncomfortable. The distance between them felt as though it had shrunk. His arm reached out of its own accord as if to touch her. His hand closed on air. She laughed.

Instinct was beginning to make itself felt. A small voice urged him to flee. *Nonsense*, he told himself. He was in no danger. This was a mere stage show, flummery. As a performer he was aware of the tricks used to pull the audience in, grab their attention. He settled himself back again, silenced the voice. Allowed his professional self to admire the man's stagecraft.

On stage, the mouth smiled, continued to whisper into Lucy's ear. Isaac could see no face even though he strained to see through the gloom, through the wisps of smoke that drifted past him from time to time. The aroma of meadows never walked through, of a harvest not gathered, assailed him. Only the finest cigars appeared to be smoked here. He failed to detect the bitter undertones.

"Ah, fresh blood," mocked the voice.

The audience laughed too and Isaac felt as if they were all looking at him. And it was more than just them. There was something else hiding within these shadows. Others not seated at the tables, others who were watching him carefully, quietly, as if he were a prize specimen to be examined.

And their interest was a cold interest. He could feel their evil. His skin crawled. Had he been brought here merely to be the butt of someone else's cruel joke? A reversal of his usual role but an apt revenge? He dismissed the fleeting thought.

He kept his eyes fixed firmly on the stage. Waiting for the show proper to begin.

"It already has," said the voice.

Now he recognised it, recalled its owner. Genesis Caul. The man who had invited him here. There was no mistaking him even though he continued to keep himself hidden.

Isaac poured himself a drink. Tossed back the brandy to steady his nerves. Waited. This was not what he'd imagined.

"Gentlemen," said the invisible compere, his body still elusive despite the focus of the spotlight. "Tonight, I have something special for you. But I need a volunteer. Who will step up?"

Around him his fellow spectators eagerly rose from their seats. *A good sign*, thought Isaac as he felt his confidence return. They would not be so willing if something dreadful were about to be perpetrated on them.

"No, no," said Genesis. "I think that for tonight's little event we will ask Isaac to join us on stage. Allow him the *full* experience, shall we say."

There was more laughter at that, and Isaac allowed himself a smile. Invisible hands clapped Isaac on his back as they propelled him towards the light.

"Welcome, Isaac," said Genesis, holding his hand out to pull him up onto the stage. It was a firm grip, a strength Isaac knew immediately he couldn't match.

"I'm glad you decided to take up my invitation. I promised you an experience beyond anything you could comprehend and now is the time. I hope you don't mind my little audience, but be assured you are amongst friends here."

A round of applause greeted these words, which Genesis acknowledged with a showman's bow.

Finally, Isaac could see the man's face. He recalled their meeting at his own little show, one that had proved less than successful, rendering Isaac embarrassed but also hungry to prove to the world what he could really do—if only they would give him a chance.

"I can help you; I can feed you. I can give you a voice," the stranger had said, and pressed his card into Isaac's hand before disappearing into that evening's small crowd.

Isaac thought of his own performance, the tricks he played on those he hypnotised. Simple, yes, but it still proved he had control. So much of his early life had been beyond his control, bringing with it so much pain and suffering that he determined never to be in that position as an adult. *He* would be the one in command. *His* would be the voice obeyed.

Revelation had come when he met Samuel Groves. A poor mesmerist but one who planted the seed of an idea into the youthful Isaac. He taught the boy everything he knew before he died. Isaac, ever impatient to learn, had no time for the niceties of an apprenticeship and Samuel had soon outlived his usefulness. Isaac barely thought of the man anymore; just another corpse rotting in London's sewers.

He took over Samuel's circuit, and nobody questioned it. People came and went all the time in the East End. He'd learned to give the audience the escape they craved from their dreary lives, discovering early on people would pay to witness the humiliation of others, and he was more than happy to provide such a show, provided the humiliation was not his own.

Genesis placed his hand on Isaac's shoulder. "Gentlemen, tonight I, Genesis Caul, will guide our dear Lucy here through the recesses of the mind of our new brother, Isaac Bercow. I trust you have no dark secrets, Brother Isaac!"

Again, the knowing laughter. They all had secrets here.

"Do not fear," said Genesis, squeezing his shoulder harder, too hard. "All who come here go through this little… *initiation*. And I do not reveal anything that is too embarrassing. I am here only to serve and entertain."

Yet the man's eyes reflected no humour, no warmth; what Isaac read there instead was greed—and hunger. He could have been looking at himself. His heart started to pound, loud to his ears; could the audience hear it? He was no coward, but he felt the edge of fear begin to creep its way through him. He pushed it back. Isaac Bercow was *not* afraid.

He permitted Genesis to guide him to the chair opposite the girl. She turned and faced him. Involuntarily he shrank back. As a doctor, Isaac dealt with death often enough on the streets of the East End and if she hadn't moved, he would have sworn she was a corpse.

"No, she has a pulse, dear *doctor*," said Genesis.

Isaac stared at Genesis; he hadn't spoken, had he? And was the man mocking him by using that title? Was Genesis aware Isaac was not much more than a barber surgeon? He thought of his lodgings and the framed certificates hanging on the wall; he was proud of those even if they were forgeries. If you live a lie long enough you end up believing it.

"Lucy," said Genesis. "Can you see the doctor?"

"Yes," she murmured, her voice young, an innocence at odds with the corruption of her appearance; her breath, fetid, foul.

"What do you see?"

She stared hard at him, forcing Isaac to shift uncomfortably beneath her gaze. Eyes as black as night enveloped him, swallowed him whole. "I see a coat bought from the pawnbroker's."

The audience laughed and Isaac felt himself flush.

"I see a shirt that belonged to another, someone..." She frowned.

The sweat trickled down Isaac's back, staining the silk shirt she referred to. He had literally taken it from another's back. *No*, he told himself. These were mere actor's tricks. Information Genesis could've got from anywhere. Even so, he squirmed in his chair.

"Someone who is no longer with us but who I sense is here in the shadows," she continued.

The audience murmured, their interest piqued.

A scent drifted around him, recognisable. Cold dread washed over him. Isaac tensed.

"Does he want to speak to us, Lucy?" asked Genesis.

"No, he says it was fair enough. He'd have done the same."

She shrugged her shoulders in exactly the nonchalant manner he remembered of Daniel.

The audience clapped its approval. Everyone relaxed, including Isaac. He allowed himself a chuckle. That had been Daniel Lightfoot all over. A pity he'd had to kill him. Would she find the others?

"Further now, Lucy," ordered Genesis.

Isaac tensed again, shivered. A draught had come from somewhere, was sliding over his skin, seeping into him, following the pulse of his life round his body, reaching up into his mind. He closed his eyes and still he saw Lucy. She was shadow now, inside his head, gliding through the memories he kept locked away from everyone, sometimes even from himself.

"Hello, Isaac," she whispered. Her tone was friendly, gentle.

"Lucy?" he queried silently.

She giggled and disappeared. A little girl playing hide-and-seek.

"Ready or not, I'm coming!" she called.

He could feel her dancing through his memories, saw her watching him as a mudlark on the Thames, as a thief, a conman, a murderer. She saw it all. And as she watched, her giggle turned to laughter, a laughter that bespoke kindred spirits. The feeling of shame, of embarrassment, left him. Instead there was only relief. He was understood and accepted. He was amongst friends.

"They do say sharing is good for the soul," murmured Lucy.

"What will you tell the audience?" he asked, by now fully accepting of this unspoken conversation.

"Oh, this," she said. And sent his days in Newgate out into the world.

"And this." She told the stories of autopsies and resurrectionists, his limited medical training, with relish. Again, the audience applauded loudly.

"And that is all," she whispered. "The rest is for Genesis. And he already knows."

Then she was gone. His head felt empty, lighter, free from the intruder. His memories his own once more, his and his alone. His body regained its previous warmth.

"And there we finish our show tonight, gentlemen. I trust you will sleep well after that last, rather graphic, tale. Remember, the mind can be a powerful and dangerous tool. It is also a fragile thing. It should be used well and used wisely. Go forth my brothers and bend the world to your will."

The lights went up and Isaac was surprised to find himself and Genesis alone.

"They don't hang around in these parts," said Genesis. "Even with the protection I can give them, they still err on the side of caution. They are but novices in my trade at the moment. An apprenticeship I hope you, too, will take up. Sit with me awhile and let us discuss that proposition I mentioned before."

Isaac sat back down and allowed Genesis to pour them both a drink. The evening had unnerved him somewhat but still he would play along.

"An admirable attitude," said Genesis, reading his thoughts. "That was what drew me to you. Your desire, your ambition, your *need* to be someone, to be more than a *little* man."

Isaac thought of the streets above, the poverty and crime, the sheer misery of life. Who would not want to be someone else, something better?

"What did you think of Lucy?" Genesis asked.

"An amazing creature," said Isaac truthfully. "A remarkable gift."

"And one I will give to you," said Genesis.

"Pardon?" He had not expected that.

"I will give you a voice—"

"I have a voice," interrupted Isaac, pride stung.

"I will give you a voice people will *listen* to, and… I will give you Lucy. Between you, you will conquer society."

Nothing was ever given for free, thought Isaac. "And the price?"

"Tonight, you sensed there were others with us, others who had gone beyond this world. They need to taste life once more; it was my promise to them. They served me well."

He recalled that wall of malevolence observing him. Here was the reckoning. "How…?"

"You can find them a place to live, you can find them new flesh, a new body. For a while it will be a little… uncomfortable. They will have to travel with you; you will have to carry them through the daylight hours. But I am hoping that as your skills build, as you allow Lucy to guide you and teach you, you will help them return."

Isaac could still sense the unbodied oppressiveness around him. The predatory watchers eyeing him greedily. His skin prickled under their intensity.

"What do you mean carry them?"

"Oh, Isaac. Have you not realised? Your mind will become their home for a little while. But do not fear; you and they are very alike. I doubt you will be able to tell where their thoughts end and yours begin."

What if he refused? He had not committed to anything by coming along to the show, had he? He had viewed this evening as a mere business opportunity, something he could walk away from at any time.

But no. This was no choice, no request. Merely a polite illusion of one. Something to soothe a man's ego. Genesis had already decided what was to be done, the path Isaac was to take. Isaac had been promised control but at that moment he knew with a certainty that he had no control over his life, not anymore. He felt no surprise at this. He'd understood long ago he would sell his soul, and today, the contract had been signed.

They came to him then, those shapes from the shadows, the mass he'd sensed lurking on the edges of his own consciousness throughout the evening. And they were so dark, those unbodied souls, so full of hate and madness, their hearts stained in pitch, branded as monsters. *His* brothers. Their whispers started almost immediately, a murmuring inside that ebbed and flowed in a tide of depravity.

"You will soon get used to each other, and this always helps," said Genesis, pushing another drink towards him. "But remember, they are my children. You must look after them as a father his sons."

Isaac had never held a belief in God or the Devil as he grew up. Early on he decided any God who made the world a living hell for innocent children was no God at all, and the Devil? He was the dark part of man, that bit inside that enjoyed the suffering of others, the torment, the greed. But now? Isaac looked into the eyes of Genesis, saw many shades within, movements that bespoke a million souls in torment. And the man carried them easily.

"You see I have more to give," whispered Genesis. "I am legion. Be careful not to disappoint me.

Chapter Two

Roll up, roll up, thought Isaac as he looked at his list of patients for the next week. *Come one, come all. See what I can do for you; let me fulfil all of your desires. Roll up, roll up!*

He smiled as he scanned the list. Every consultation was a performance, when his words would dance in the dark, wrapping themselves around the unsuspecting mind until the tendrils of the thoughts he planted rooted and took hold, sowing themselves on the ceaseless tongues of society's matrons. And so they went forth and multiplied, bringing a tide of the world-weary, the heart-sore, the restless and rootless in a continual ebb and flow. Fortune and fame beckoned and still he was not satisfied.

Genesis had been right when he said Isaac would not notice the presence of those whose spirits he carried, although occasionally he felt the weight of them. They would sometimes push forward during a consultation or at an exhibition eager to see if the person in front would be a suitable home for one of them. But so far, he had held them within him. Genesis had told him that Lucy would decide who would be chosen. So, he waited.

Lucy. His assistants had raised no eyebrows at her appearance and subsequent absorption into their lives. Isaac had done what he always did. Directed their thoughts in the way he wanted. Tricks he'd used before he met Genesis.

He told them she was his niece. An orphan left to the mercy of the street until he rediscovered her. Now she no longer wore rags, although she had a distinct dislike for cleanliness. He left it to Susanna and Mary to bathe her and keep her presentable. This had been a battle, but in the end they came to a mutual agreement that Lucy only needed to bathe when she was required for a show.

She was happy to just sit there during the day, rarely moving from the stool by the often-cold fireplace, her eyes empty, vacant. As he became accustomed to her presence, he gradually realised Lucy was not where he thought she was. She would speak to him in his head as she had done that evening with Genesis and she would tell him of Susanna's and Mary's little adventures and of Dominic's shady dealings.

That was when he realised she had entered his mind once more and was doing the same to those around her. She was travelling the streets of London and seeing it through the eyes of others, building her knowledge, learning everything of Isaac's world. Learning everything he knew and more. It was a disconcerting thought.

Night was a different story unless there was a performance. She would leave the rooms in the darkest of hours to places kept from him. Perhaps she returned to Genesis, to appear before others as she had before him. He understood then she hadn't been given to him after all, had merely been loaned.

Yet through her things began to change. The relentless stream of the flotsam and jetsam of human misery arriving at his door increasingly yielded the occasional pearl, which he would hoard as jealously as any miser. The remainder, the dross, he would continue to use to deepen his knowledge, develop his expertise.

There was no lack of subjects, willing or otherwise; all were desperate to change their lives, climb out of the cesspits they inhabited, throw off the shackles of their poverty and destitution. Isaac promised to raise them up.

And so they came, extending his influence even further. And still he was not satisfied. He wanted more, so much more, and it wasn't just money or influence he craved. He wanted control. Complete and absolute control.

"I'll give you that," said Lucy. "But now it is time to start with the others. Genesis has decided your Doctor Llewellyn is to become the home of one of those you carry with you."

The voices in his head clamoured loudly when they heard her speak, each one keen to be the first to be released. His head pounded under the building pressure.

He glanced at his watch in irritation. Llewellyn was late. For a moment he wondered if the doctor had begun to suspect his true intentions. No. The man was an excellent physician, but he lacked imagination.

Isaac almost regretted his decision to use his friend in this way, almost but not quite. The pursuit of progress, of truth, demanded sacrifice. He also needed to relieve his own mental suffering. He had to free whatever monsters resided in himself at any cost.

His frown deepened as he looked at the latest medical journals. His paper hadn't made any of them although his name had been mentioned in the editorial column and it hadn't been very complimentary. They needed to leave their ivory towers and really see what he could do. Isaac knew he had to keep his impatience in check, allow his plans to fall into place.

By word of mouth, Isaac's reputation was growing. He and Lucy cured society's darlings of fainting fits and neurosis, their sons and heirs of speech impediments and weakness of character, and all through the power of his voice—*his* voice and Lucy's unique ability to roam the neural pathways of others.

He achieved what potions and pills could not, allowing his patients to slough off their sufferings and return to those circles where they were no longer shunned but courted and admired.

To have that power over others, to control and manipulate, made him feel omnipotent. All he needed now was to show in public what he was capable of, move his stage into the upper echelons. He hoped that his more respectable client base would ease his path, but so far the Society had refused to grant him membership, dismissing him as a dilettante, not a *real* man of science. It rankled but soon he would change their minds, literally if he had to.

Doctor Rees Llewellyn was his first step to achieving the desired recognition, even as he was at the same time the unwitting subject of one of Isaac's most challenging experiments, the one experiment no one could know about; this was to be the start of his repayments to Genesis.

He'd shown the Whitechapel doctor his research papers, his subjects; allowed him to observe consultations, his patients, study Lucy. Together they walked the streets and saw the results of his treatment in action. In Europe, eminent physicians had submitted to leading scientific journals on the same field of study but even so Llewellyn continued to deny the efficacy of hypnotherapy, just as the Society for Psychical Research had.

The sound of voices interrupted his thoughts. Dominic, his assistant, opened the door to admit the other doctor, the *real* doctor. They indulged in idle chat whilst drinks were poured and cigars lit before they returned yet again to the argument that continued between them.

"There is something dark and evil lurking in the recesses of every human mind," said Isaac dispassionately. "All it needs is a door to be opened and it is free."

"And you would prefer this… this darkness to be unshackled? That man should be allowed to indulge his baser instincts *without censure*!"

Isaac sighed. Llewellyn could prove surprisingly unimaginative at times.

"Imagine an engine—or a kettle—if you will, either example will suffice."

Llewellyn turned away from the fire and focussed his still doubtful look on Isaac. "Yes, yes," he said irritably. "Water boils in both and steam is produced."

"What happens then if there is no room for the steam to escape?"

Llewellyn frowned. "That's schoolboy science. The pressure would build up and there would be an explosion."

"And do you not think," said Isaac, "that the evil residing in man, that dark stain, that blemish on the heart, will not continue to grow and fester, building up such a pressure on the conscience that in the end its owner can only explode, indulge his violent sensibilities in the most extreme manner possible?"

"So, you would allow a lesser evil to avoid a greater crime?"

Isaac nodded.

"You make it sound as though you are merely lancing a boil," said Llewellyn. "But you are playing with a man's soul. And who's to say that the lesser evil will not feed into something greater? You tread dangerous ground."

"All I am doing is giving them the freedom to be who they truly are. I unlock their minds—"

"Back to that again," said Llewellyn in exasperation. "A clever trick. You use that girl and pretend she can enter the minds of others, read what is in their hearts, what ails their bodies. It is all mere suggestion. I am not sure you can claim any true clinical value in what you do."

That rankled. "Think of the mentally disturbed, the neurotics, the hysterical. Think how easy and how much more humane such a treatment would be. Poor souls whose only future would be in Bedlam would be allowed to return to society, become useful, sober, respectable members."

"But you could never be certain," said Llewellyn at last. "How would you know if your influence had worn off and they were not just hiding behind a mask, waiting for the moment when they could reveal their true selves. *That black stain you speak of?*"

Isaac swirled his port, watched the glow of the fire reflect off the cut crystal. His earlier feeling of satisfaction had vanished, replaced by a creeping irritation at Llewellyn's refusal to give sufficient credence to his work.

Usually so accepting of Isaac's theories, Llewellyn was being remarkably immovable on this particular topic. He stubbornly ignored the evidence of Isaac's successes, clung to the belief no man could control another in the manner he described. Only God had that power. *Was Isaac claiming to be God?*

No, not God, *a* God. Isaac was no Christian despite his attendance at church, a bit of playacting to underline his respectability. God had not been there for him as a child. Only a void; bleak, dark, and silent. If he ever heard a voice at all it was his own. He had no wish to be subject to the rules and morals of others.

What was morality but another form of subjugation? A repression brought about by another person's viewpoint or beliefs, followed only because of long tradition supported by those in power, those with wealth for whom it served the purpose of maintaining the status quo, maintaining their own privileged position.

Isaac played along and would continue to do so until the doors had opened for him and he was allowed the stage he required. After that, tradition or no, he would follow his own path.

He did not wish to leave the comfort of his hearth but there was someone, a former patient, he could show to his friend. Lucy had been inventive with that one.

"You need more than a few tricks of the mesmerist to produce a paper the Society will take seriously," said Llewellyn, picking up one of the journals from the table and so not noticing the reaction to his dismissive reference.

So far, Isaac had kept the doctor blissfully unaware of the true extent of his research, his experiments, the lives infiltrated, controlled—including Llewellyn's own. The time was fast approaching when Llewellyn would finally become aware of what was really happening and how tightly Isaac had bound him in his spider's web of deceit. Llewellyn would rail and protest, of that he was sure, but there was nothing he could do about it.

Isaac would—could—never release him. He was his first Host. The carrier. There were some aspects that had to remain hidden from the good doctor, at least for the time being. Isaac had more experiments to perform, more results to gather. His paper would be unique. The Society could not ignore him then. It was also a debt he owed to Genesis Caul.

"Don't worry, my friend," said Isaac. "Everything will be documented with the utmost rigour. I will not embarrass you. Now come, I have something I am sure will interest you."

An expression of regret passed over Llewellyn's face as he abandoned his drink and stubbed out his cigar. His reluctance to leave this brief respite from the miserable world of his patients was clear. Yet the doctor still followed Isaac dutifully out onto the misty streets of Whitechapel Road.

Isaac, too, was ill-at-ease. There was a stirring within his mind, a shifting, pulsing force that would not rest. His own little black stain seeping its way up towards the light, demanding its release.

Isaac welcomed the anonymity the fog-shrouded night brought; it hid his discomposure as thoughts that had lain dormant during the day shifted and pushed their way to the forefront of his consciousness. These were his brothers—as he now called them— bequeathed by Genesis over a year ago, rising up towards the light, demanding their release, feeding his theories and research, bringing with them, however, an even greater hunger.

And this hunger had a voice that at times threatened to devour his sanity, yet at other times lay there quietly, like now, listening as he spoke to Llewellyn. Then they would murmur and whisper, rising up from inside his consciousness, taking form, hidden spectators watching the world from behind his eyes. There was one voice in particular that rose above the others, was more demanding, more insistent.

It was this voice Isaac would gift to Llewellyn, where the unsuspecting doctor would nurture it in the dark until it had as much power over his earthly body as Llewellyn's own self. In time, like the proverbial cuckoo in the nest, Llewellyn in the original form would cease to exist, absorbed completely by Isaac's parasite.

The good doctor was unaware of Isaac's ultimate aim. Inspired by Genesis, Isaac was determined to isolate the conscience of another from its body, remove it from its skin-bound home, understand its true nature. Just as Genesis had with Lucy; he intended to do the same. He was near his goal now. Soon...

"Are you sure?" asked a voice. *"Do you really believe you are so powerful, so clever to achieve such a feat? How do you not know that perhaps you might be deluded... even mad?"*

Madness? No, definitely not; his pride would not allow him to entertain such a thought. It was method, that was all, something missing that led to his inability to control this final stage. That was something he would have to work on before he performed such a feat in public. He had known Genesis was watching him in his endeavours; Lucy informed him of that. But there had been no disapproval. And so, he continued his efforts.

Meanwhile, every day it was becoming harder to shut out the voices of the unanchored spirits, their ceaseless pleading for a return to life, to a fleshly form. The stain was growing and demanding its release.

It had started to cross Isaac's mind that maybe these entities might find a way to infiltrate his own body permanently, seep into his own mind. He woke each morning with a growing feeling of dread that one day somebody else would be looking out from behind his eyes. He needed another carrier to take the risk away from himself. Llewellyn would be the start.

"Go on," whispered the voice that spoke above others, urging him on. *"Give him to me. I promise I'll behave."*

A raucous cry drew him back to his surroundings. They were not alone. Around them shapes and shadows emerged from the mist, following them along the slick pavement, crowding around them briefly before leaving them behind and swirling on into the night.

Isaac and Llewellyn continued in their wake. It seemed as if the whole of Whitechapel was headed for the same spot. When they reached the Silver King's penny gaff, Llewellyn raised an eyebrow.

"This is where you will show me your incontrovertible proof?"

"Yes. But I will not tell you what to expect. I want you to just watch and make up your own mind. I will not try and influence you."

Llewellyn laughed. "Then I suppose I must be thankful for small mercies."

Chapter Three

Isaac guided Llewellyn to a spot on the stairs where he would be free to enjoy the show without the danger of getting his pocket picked. Henry, one of the Silver King's men, would keep an eye on him.

Meanwhile, Isaac watched the Friday night gathering with an expert eye. The crowd pushed and jostled with apparent good humour, but long experience had taught him the mood could change at any minute; an undercurrent of violence bubbled ever-present just beneath the surface. Despite his aversion, he knew he could never leave this world completely behind him. Its moods and caprices, its dirt and stench had infiltrated his own heart even as he sought to distance himself from it.

"Are you sure about this?" asked Tom Norman, joining him at the window. "It's been a good partnership, made us both a lot of money."

This was the first parting of ways, a necessary step towards his greater goal. He no longer needed this training ground; Lucy agreed. Isaac smiled at his soon-to-be-former partner.

"And will continue to make you money. You knew this arrangement was only temporary," he said.

"But if there's trouble?" continued Tom.

"Then I will come," said Isaac, knowing Tom was worried some of his money-spinners might, quite literally, come to their senses. So far, he had not determined a time limit on any of his subjects. Ideas and suggestions implanted a year ago continued to exert a strength of control surprising even to him. Tonight, Llewellyn would be able to observe one such example.

Tom had been a good friend, a rarity in this dark corner of the East End. In his position as an entertainer, a presenter of the novel, he'd accepted Isaac's ideas and suggestions with alacrity, his business acumen realising the possibilities of what Isaac proposed, and indeed, delivered. It was Tom who provided Isaac with the pathetic specimens that allowed him to hone and perfect his skills.

"I'm glad to see Mrs Baker is on the bill tonight," said Isaac.

"Always a good 'un to pull in the crowds," said Tom.

A self-satisfied smile crept across Isaac's face. Her regular appearances at Tom's chain of penny gaffs were testament to the influence he continued to exert over her.

Llewellyn appeared at his side and Isaac made the necessary introductions.

"Your friend has a truly remarkable gift," said Tom.

"He has some talent, I will allow," admitted Llewellyn, somewhat grudgingly, Isaac thought.

"I'm afraid Llewellyn still entertains some doubts as to the power of hypno-suggestion."

Tom raised his eyebrows. "Then tonight Mrs Baker will vanquish your doubts forever," he said theatrically.

"There is nothing this man"—here Tom paused to indicate Isaac—"cannot get another to do. He has the power to control the thoughts, the feelings, the actions—the very soul—of another in ways we cannot comprehend. We should be thankful these unique abilities reside in one such as him and not in those who seek to benefit from the misfortunes of others."

Isaac gave Tom a look. The man was overdoing it somewhat and what were they doing tonight if not benefitting from another's misery?

Thankfully, Llewellyn appeared to be more interested in the crowds below him than in Tom's flowery speech.

"How long has it been now?" asked Tom.

"At least a year, I should say," said Isaac.

"Mrs Baker," explained Isaac to Llewellyn. "She's on the bill tonight."

"And she still has no idea?" said Tom.

"None," said Isaac.

"And her husband?"

"Still perfectly happy to take the money," said Isaac.

It was becoming livelier outside; the costers were not a crowd known for their reticence. With money in their pockets, they sought escape from the hardship of the daily grind. Boys and girls as young as eight or nine mingled with youths and toothless crones, mimicking their foul language and lewd behaviour. There was no such thing as an innocent child in this part of the world.

The murky lamplight cast its unforgiving glow over those nearest the door. The wretchedness of these folk never ceased to disgust him, but they had been useful. And the beauty of it had been they hadn't even realised.

"I'm glad you never hypnotised me," said Tom, laughing, as he headed towards the stairs.

Oh yes, Tom had indeed been a very willing participant, mused Isaac as he and Llewellyn followed him.

Isaac took Llewellyn to his usual vantage point on such nights. Hidden by tattered canvas rags that served as stage curtains, he could watch the evening's entertainment unobserved.

Once upon a time he, too, had performed down there although in a different guise; now he hid behind curtains in order to preserve his anonymity. It was common for the occasional toff to slum it in these parts, allowing them to give free rein to their own baser instincts or to simply come and observe so they could shock polite society with tales of evil and degradation. Theirs was the world which Isaac had proceeded to infiltrate. It would do no good to be recognised and denounced at some future date as a mere street performer. The cloak of respectability meant everything.

By now, the boards that fronted the shop had been removed, opening up the audience space for the crowds who surged forward.

Tom Norman, the Silver King himself, stood halfway down the stairs so all could see him.

"Welcome, welcome, ladies and gentlemen," he roared, adding with a knowing wink, "and I use that term loosely."

Raucous laughter greeted his comments.

"Come on, your Majesty, don't go complimentin' your paying subjects now, you know it won't wash." More laughter.

And in they came; some barefoot and half-clothed but still with the wherewithal to buy a pot of porter as it did the rounds, seeking oblivion from their miserable lives. Already the lads were eyeing up prospective partners, making obscene comments to the chosen girls who responded with delighted laughter. Worn bonnets and frayed feathers bobbed in time to the piano that had just struck up, even as a likely lad stole his arm beneath his girl's shawl.

There was a scuffle as some latecomers pushed and shoved their way to the front, a couple of the youths jumping on shoulders and walking across the crowd to much cursing and annoyance from the men and older women as the younger girls giggled and shrieked in admiration, the unattached hoping to be noticed by these daring types.

Whilst the dismal lighting within could hide many faults, it could not mask the smell of the crowd, their stench floating up to Isaac and forcing him to bury his face briefly in a scented handkerchief. Once, he would not have noticed but as he had moved further and further away from this world, so his immunity to such things lessened.

A cracked voice broke out from the stage.

"Don't stop my 'arf a pint of beer,

It's the only fing what's keepin' me alive ... "

"Well, it certainly ain't your singin' voice," piped up an onlooker.

"Reckon you need a drink now," shouted out another.

"You're not wrong, pal!" responded the singer, laughing, as Tom handed him a tankard with a flourish. He downed it quickly and then, with a belch that earned a roar of approval, not to mention admiring comments, he returned to his song.

"I don't mind yer stoppin' my coffee and my tea,

But 'arf a pint of beer, is medicine to me."

More applause thundered through the small building. Isaac could feel it rumbling through the boards beneath his feet.

It was the next act he had come to see. She was the first he presented to the public and the longest-serving of his and Lucy's guinea pigs. If he ever needed to remind himself of what he could get others to do by force of will, she was the act he would come to watch. He could see Llewellyn's focussed attention, knew he was watching the stage.

"Ladies an' gen'lemen," said Tom, now centre stage. "We all know when times is 'ard that we'll eat anyfin' that'll keep us goin'."

He paused as a covered cage was brought up and placed beside him.

"'Ow many of you 'owever would care to dine on these little blighters?"

He removed the blanket with a flourish, revealing four scrawny looking rats scrabbling at the bars of their prison.

"And furthermore, 'ow many of you would be so desperate as to eat 'em raw?"

"Probably tastes a lot better than my missus's cooking," called one to general hilarity.

"Well tonight we are joined by the redoubtable Mrs Baker, who will demonstrate how, exactly, these little edibles are best ingested."

Mrs Baker came onto the stage then to a huge round of applause. Tom Norman pulled out the chair for her, as regular as any waiter; she sat down with a smile and demurely placed her hands in her lap. The table in front of her was covered with a pure white tablecloth. This was always burned after, but Tom insisted on its whiteness; it gave a much stronger contrast to the contents of her meal. A place setting had been laid but she would not use the knife and fork, there was no need.

She considered the cage for a moment, as if deciding which rat to choose first. She did not speak and kept her focus on the creatures. After a short pause, Tom opened the cage door, and Mrs Baker removed her glove and placed her exposed hand inside.

Disgusted squeals from the coster girls greeted her action as the rats sniffed and butted against her flesh. Then she picked up a small, dirty white specimen and lifted him out.

"Ladies and gentlemen, this is just for starters!" said Tom.

Mrs Baker surveyed her audience with a faint, but distant, smile. Then she turned her gaze once more to the rat, opened her mouth, and bit its head off. It took a few attempts to take the head completely off, but she achieved it.

The audience looked on in shocked horror; one or two girls at the front fainted, another ran out the nearest exit and was promptly sick. All were disgusted yet could not bear to tear their eyes away from the revolting sight. Blood ran in dribbles down Mrs Baker's chin, spattering onto the virgin cloth. The crunch of bones could clearly be heard over the silent audience.

It usually took a lot to hush the mob but now you could've heard a pin drop. Fascination overcame revulsion and when she finished, they cried out for more. At the end of the act, four headless corpses lay neatly on the plate. Mrs Baker dabbed delicately at the corners of her mouth, smearing the blood across her cheek, then rose and bowed to the audience.

Isaac noted the vague quality of her eyes, the absence of emotion, still as strong as ever. He would have to release her from his spell soon, however; he'd noticed the difficulty with which she had attacked the rat. Her teeth were getting worn out. He wasn't sure how Mr Baker would take it; the man had got used to living off his wife. He would have to get off his fat backside and earn a penny for a change.

From the moment she had appeared on the stage, Llewellyn had concentrated avidly on the woman. Looks of disgust and horror had crossed over his face as Isaac knew they would but then they'd been replaced by an expression of total fascination; he was just the same as the audience.

"You did this," Llewellyn said.

It was not a question, merely a simple statement of fact.

"You have made her a freak of nature, a monster. When you first introduced me to your work, you said it would be for their betterment, that they would be able to improve their condition in society."

"And that is what I have done," said Isaac. "Before, they never had a penny to rub together. She walked the streets, immoral, in the grip of vice. Her husband would accost the men she solicited, steal whatever they possessed that she hadn't already taken. Now she bites the heads off a few rats and earns more in one night than she would in a month of streetwalking. Less harm all round."

"And it makes you money as well," said Llewellyn, looking at him with disapproval.

"What I make, I use to fund my research," said Isaac. "Do you now admit to the power of hypnotism over the human psyche?"

"Yes," said Llewellyn grudgingly. "Although I had hoped to see it put to a more fitting use."

"That," said Isaac, "is something I can promise you. Now come, we have work to do, you and I."

He led Llewellyn down a back staircase and out into a side alley; across the street they could see the hustle and bustle of London Hospital. Frequently the clientele of this particular gaff would find themselves across the road having overindulged or come to harm in the regular brawls that occurred on such nights.

They walked down Whitechapel Road, expertly dodging the pickpockets who worked there, ignoring the girls who plied their trade in the shadows. That was something he had taught Llewellyn long ago.

"Where are we going?" asked Llewellyn breathlessly as he sought to keep up with Isaac.

"We have an appointment to keep," said Isaac. Speed would help confuse Llewellyn.

Isaac took a left turn, then a right, then another left. They were deep into the Rookeries by now. He found the door he was looking for, black peeling paint and warped frames, and pushed it open. It was too misshapen for the lock to work but that didn't matter.

He moved through a bare hallway and came to another door at the far end. This one was well-built and solid. It was also secured with a heavy-duty padlock in addition to the usual lock. Once inside, the bolts added further security.

Whilst the rest of the house looked as though it were literally on its last legs, the rooms he rented were dry and comfortable. He had paid out for repairs to the beams and plasterwork and glazed the windows, although taking care to fit shutters to prevent their breaking. He had also positioned one or two little mantraps around the place to discourage any would-be burglars. Only one man had attempted a break-in, he'd had to have a leg amputated.

"A strange place for a consultation," said Llewellyn, looking around him.

Isaac bolted the door behind them and lit a lamp. He pulled out a silver watch from his waistcoat pocket. It was a heavy specimen, engraved with an intricate pattern of truly remarkable craftsmanship. The silver glinted in the golden glow of the flickering flame, sending its wavering shadow onto the wall as it spun and danced in the gentle light.

The watch had been his father's. He had stolen it on the day he left home.

Now he let it continue its dance, watching Llewellyn as he did so. He would not speak yet; it would break the spell.

Slowly he swung the watch back and forth, back and forth, its path already being followed by Llewellyn, completely unaware of anything else around him. Isaac had conditioned him as well as he had conditioned Mrs Baker, but he still reinforced his treatment on a regular basis.

Llewellyn stood, as still as any statue. Tall and solid, he was a reassuring figure, as indeed a doctor and surgeon that served this community needed to be. Only thirty-five, his thick brown hair was already edged with silver, adding to his overall air of distinguished respectability in stark contrast to his surroundings. The man had never experienced the want that had infected Isaac's own upbringing, never known the violence and suffering meted out at the hand of an unforgiving father, the shame of a mother who sold herself for the price of a drink.

At the gaff earlier, Isaac said he would not seek to influence Llewellyn. But that had been a half-truth, applying only to the performance they'd been watching. For some time now he had been conditioning the man without his knowledge, realising a latent susceptibility in the good doctor, creating room for something— someone—of whom the doctor was completely unaware. Isaac had decided not to wait any longer; he could not afford the risk to his own position, his own sanity.

"There," he said to the squatter in his mind, the one who had shouted loudest all evening. "His body is yours completely now… on one condition."

"Which is?"

"Llewellyn exists by day, you… you must keep your activities to the night, hidden in the dark, in the mist."

A small part of Isaac felt some shame at what he was doing to his friend, but the desire to rid himself of this dominance in his mind was too great and easily overcame his finer feelings. Besides, it would be an interesting experiment, seeing how far you could compel someone to commit acts that went completely against their morals and everything that was decent. He always looked for the advantage in everything.

"I trust you find your new home satisfactory," said Isaac, continuing the pendulum motion of his watch.

Llewellyn leered in the strange light, his mouth drooping and eyes squinting, stance changing so he stooped slightly, forming a grotesque out of respectability.

"Evening, boss," he said, tipping his hat as he did so. "Must say I'm feelin' better already. Bein' cooped up in that brain of yours wasn't doin' me any good at all."

"The feeling's mutual," said Isaac. "But remember my condition. I don't want you compromising Llewellyn in any way. He's a respectable man, a good doctor. You look after him."

"Oh, I will," said the other. "I will."

Isaac moved over to a small cupboard and pulled out a gin bottle and two glasses.

"A toast," he said as he passed a glass to Llewellyn. "To our enterprise this night."

They saluted each other and emptied their glasses.

"Now to business."

Llewellyn's intruder was engaged in something much more likely to draw protests and defiance from the subconscious. Isaac had to know how far he could push another human being act against all accepted moral codes of behaviour. This had nothing to do with the lesser evil. He watched as Llewellyn prepared himself.

"You have everything?"

Llewellyn opened out the folds of his cape to reveal an inside pocket containing some lethal looking blades.

"You have chosen your target?"

"Aye."

"So, who is it to be? Which piece of dirt are you to clean from the streets tonight? No, don't tell me. I want to read it in the papers like everyone else."

A shrug of the shoulders. "As you like."

"And the other thing?"

A sly grin. "All in hand. Just what the doctor ordered."

They both laughed at that. Isaac would have to remember who he was now, learn to respond to the title which he bequeathed on himself. He had no papers, but should anyone demand to see them or ask for a reference—well, he had that under control.

"Listen," said Isaac, serious once more. "This is important work you are doing."

Llewellyn nodded and Isaac let him go off into the night before returning to his lodging house to prepare for his readings the next day. He also had a letter to write. It would be interesting to hear what the Academy thought of his latest paper.

Outside, the fog swirled, hiding the tall, cloaked figure as it made its way along muffled streets, searching for that which needed cleansing. Llewellyn had work to do.

Isaac closed the door behind him with a sigh of relief. He always felt this way after visiting Whitechapel Road, but the place was a necessary evil, drawing him back with its endless possibilities. There he was King, no, not King, God. He controlled and directed the lives of so many, and they didn't even know it; he decided who lived, and yes, who died. They swirled about him in their fight for survival, the vulnerable, the mad, the criminal, and he had risen above them all.

Even these rooms would soon belong to his past. He despised the poverty they projected, claiming him as an inmate with their bare boards and ill-fitting windows, a stark contrast to the new lodgings that awaited him. However, he would not break the link, not just yet; the location was necessary for his work with Llewellyn.

With an effort he cleared his mind of both men; it was time to focus on Mrs Wintringham.

This worthy matron had been his first step on the path he travelled. It had taken him some time to find her. Many women on the lower rungs of society had failed to meet his requirements but Mrs Wintringham, oh, Mrs Wintringham.

She was a find. Middle-aged and querulous, semi-abandoned by a husband who spent a lot of time in India—he could understand why the man wanted to keep so much distance between himself and his wife.

Tomorrow, he would be conducting a consultation at her home in Holborn, a more genteel area than the one in which he currently operated. There he would be displaying another aspect of his talents.

Susanna, his assistant at these events, had obtained a list of the expected guests by gossiping with the servants below stairs. Resourcefully, she'd also discovered the names of others not on the list but who had a tendency to 'pop in.' His knowledge of these women in particular would surely boost the credulity of his audience, should they choose to visit. Of course, he had Lucy, but he did not want to be completely reliant upon that creature. He did not trust her or Genesis.

"*Very wise, Doctor*," said a distant voice.

Isaac surveyed the papers on his desk and proceeded to transcribe the information onto index cards and then commit those details to memory. He had always been blessed with a powerful and retentive mind, something that made the task easier.

Mrs Wintringham herself was a very indiscreet creature, offering up little nuggets of information about any who stood above her in the upper echelons of society. By name-dropping she thought to impress those who listened, and this was true of the circles in which she mixed—where all shared the same pathetic desperateness to climb the slippery rungs of advancement; whilst it did not impress Isaac, it did add to his store of knowledge. Soon he would introduce these matrons to Lucy. Then he would really start making his name.

Isaac put his work away and sat by the dying fire. There was no need to stoke the flames higher; the green liquid he swirled in his glass would give him all the warmth he needed. He leaned back in his chair and allowed the heat to spread through him, closing his eyes against the world around him and turning his focus inwards.

Chapter Four

Llewellyn, imprisoned in his own mind by the stranger Isaac had gifted, could only look on helplessly as his captor strode along the labyrinthine maze that was Whitechapel, ignoring all salutations, every beggar's plea, intent only on reaching Winthrop Street.

He tried to speak, arouse the conscience that was his against the intruder but was forced back into his own hell, a helpless bystander to whatever was to come. The voice came back, mocked him, tormented him.

Preparation, my dear doctor, is the key. You will carry me to the tools I need in order to test Dr Bercow's theories. Tonight, I am the scientist—that should please you—the man who requires the proof of his own eyes. I will allow you to observe my experiments, but I will not let you interfere.

How far could one man push another? Isaac Bercow had declared he could free the dark stain that lay hidden in the depths of every human mind. Had he really released that which lurked inside Llewellyn or was it merely some drug, administered for Bercow's own sadistic amusement? *Who was in control now?* Llewellyn wondered as he continued to make his way deeper into the shadows of London.

Few lamps had been lit to lift the gloom, despite the lateness of the hour and the depth of the fog, but perhaps it was just as well. The sight that would have been revealed to the passer-by was guaranteed to turn even the strongest of stomachs. Instead, everything remained cloaked in mystery, an adventure of strange shapes and monstrous distortions that loomed out briefly before fading back. The night had its own population, and they were busy as always.

For the moment though, Llewellyn and his parasite trod their way between the ethereal shapeshifters, completely at home on the villainous streets. Even if he had been blind—and Llewellyn had not yet been deprived of his sight—he would have found his way easily enough to their intended destination. Like a hound, the parasite was following a scent; stronger, ever stronger, it drew them on.

Oh, Doctor. What delights lie ahead of us? Can you feel your heart race, your pulse throb with desire? That longing...

The reek of the building assaulted Llewellyn before he saw it, leaving no doubt as to the line of business carried out on these premises but Isaac's monster was free within him and this stink was mere sweet perfume. And all he could do was watch.

Harrison, Barber & Co. Ltd. was just one of a number of slaughterhouses in the area. The huge gates were unlocked as he knew they would be at this late hour. There were many who worked these unearthly shifts, performing tasks that were better hidden from the hardiest souls.

He walked carefully, sneaking along the walls like the thief he was about to become, trying to avoid the dark rivulets running across the courtyard, gathering in pools to congeal in the night air. He trod in something soft and slippery but refused to even contemplate its origin; it was of no consequence.

Lights shone out from work sheds where the main act of butchery was performed. He peered in, taking care to conceal himself from view. He could see Harry already sharpening his knife and axe, ready to set to work on the next creature.

The parasite had watched Harry at work many times when Isaac had brought Llewellyn here in one of the trances that had allowed him to travel freely for a change—before he had taken up permanent residence. He no longer had to listen to the other voices that howled and shrieked in continual torment within Isaac's own mind; he still, however, had to listen to Genesis as did all creatures on God's—and the Devil's—earth.

Together they had listened to the song of the axe, the melody of the knife, the fear in the animal's cries, all of which was music to their ears. The creature had been thankful of the doctor's own small skill in the art of minor surgery, but nothing compared to the sheer theatre demonstrated by the slaughtermen. Here were men whose skill and finesse he grew to admire, and he determined to replicate their stagecraft in his own actions.

The sound of hooves drew the intruder's attention. Someone was coming into the courtyard. Cautiously, he moved back into the shadows as he saw Charley Brittain leading in an old nag.

"Got a live one for you tonight, Harry," he called.

The summons brought Harry to the entrance and the massive doors were pushed further apart so more light spilled out into the blackness. Llewellyn allowed himself to be pressed deeper into the shelter of the wall. All free movement, free will, had vanished; he could only watch events unfold.

By now, Harry had taken off his bloodied apron and put his tools aside before he moved forward to greet his victim. For a person who meted out death on a regular basis, he was surprisingly sensitive to the feelings of these dumb creatures.

He stood in front of the horse, a poor broken-down old specimen, and gently stroked its nose.

"Hello, old fella," he said. "Time for you to rest, eh?"

The horse whickered softly and took a piece of apple from the man's hand, its whiskers tickling his palm.

"Come on, Harry," said Charley impatiently. "We ain't got all night."

They both laughed at that, knowing that that was precisely what they had got. Theirs was the work of the dark.

"Alright, old fella," said Harry. "Why don't you come along with me?"

The horse trustingly followed Harry into the abattoir. Charley tethered the horse as Harry once more donned his apron and picked up the long thin blade. The horse started to move nervously as it scented the blood on Harry's apron, but Harry reached out his hand and patted the animal on its neck, crooning softly to soothe it once more.

As he stood stroking the animal, Charley came over and swiftly hacked off the mane and tail, and all the time Harry continued to sing to the poor beast. Even when they put the shade over his eyes so the creature would remain calm for the next stage, Harry sang and the horse remained still. Then Charley handed him his axe and in one smooth movement, Harry delivered the death blow.

There was a heavy thud as the animal fell lifeless to the floor, but, even then, Harry reached over and gave him a final caress.

"Poor old fella," he murmured.

"For gawd's sake, 'arry'," said Charley. "You're gettin' bleedin' soft in the 'ead."

Harry looked up at his workmate and smiled. "Nah," he said. "Just hopin' I get treated gently like when it's my turn to go."

Charley snorted. "I'll see to it personally," he said. "Now get a bleedin' move on."

Together they fixed the animal's hooves to chains and hoisted him up from the ground. Then silently and methodically, they flayed the hide from the horse before deftly and expertly carving the meat from the bone to leave just the skeleton, white and ghostly, hanging above them whilst around their feet blood flowed.

Llewellyn could feel the monster's excitement at what they had just witnessed, the awe it inspired as the men went about their business, his own mission currently forgotten.

To kill in such a manner and with so much expertise is truly remarkable, is it not, Doctor? As a fellow professional, you must admire their skill. We will become their disciples, Doctor. Tonight, we will perform in their honour. A tribute is demanded.

Llewellyn's eyes were forced back to the men, busy dispatching the bones into vats for boiling. Discarded tools and apron lay unattended nearby. Silently, stealthily, he crept in and retrieved the items before once more returning to the darkness.

Just what we need, eh, Doctor? Don't want to get our fine clothes messy now, do we? That really would draw a comment. And I have more than one experiment I wish to perform before you get caught.

Caught?

Sadly, yes. Personally, I would have spared you that, but you upset Doctor Bercow, you know. He thinks you look down on him—don't deny it now, I can read you like a book.

But surely you don't want to get caught, whispered Llewellyn.

As I said, it is you who will get caught. I have been promised another… um, residency when it is time to leave.

Unable to protest, Llewellyn slipped the apron on beneath his coat. Wearing such a garment was common at this time of night when the butchers and slaughterhouses were a hive of activity—and there were so many of them in this area.

He left Winthrop Street and meandered up and down Whitechapel Road, pausing outside London Hospital and remembering his earlier visit.

Then, the parasite had been a prisoner to Isaac, now he had his freedom, although it would have been much better without the sanctimonious Doctor Llewellyn muttering in his ear every five seconds. The man had no control over his body but his thoughts were there, his silly little morals, lurking in the background, taking the edge off his fun; he hadn't been able to shut him up completely—yet. Perhaps it was time to give the doctor something to moan about.

The hospital seemed to be doing a good trade in treating the drunk and disorderly. It was always the same on a Friday night, when wages went on drink before all else. He needed somewhere quieter to find his mark.

A woman came ambling towards him, slightly unsteady.

"Evenin', Nellie," he said, recognising her as she stepped into the embrace of the gaslight, rolling the sound of the smoother tones of Llewellyn around in his mouth. Much better than his terrible Russian accent, more in keeping with the area, more inclined to promote trust—and respect. Genesis had certainly given him a prize.

Her eyes widened in surprise but then Nellie smiled as she recognised the doctor.

"Evenin', Doc," she said. "Out on your rounds?"

"Not tonight, Nellie," said Llewellyn. "I am just out for a constitutional."

She looked at him in puzzlement that he should choose such a place to walk for leisure, then she broke into a leering grin, distorting her face into an ugly grimace. He shuddered; not with fear, noticed Llewellyn, but with growing excitement.

"Not tonight, eh, sir?" she cackled. "What you after then?"

He did not answer.

Llewellyn breathed a sigh of relief. Perhaps there would be no bloodletting.

On the contrary, my dear doctor. We will come back to this creature another time. Unfortunately, this isn't quite the right location for what I have in mind. You can read my thoughts, can't you?

And he showed them to Llewellyn who shrank back in fear and terror.

"Too embarrassed, are we, dearie? Single gent with no wife to tend to his needs. I could see you right."

He stepped back.

Nellie shrugged. "Suit yerself. But you won't find many of us around tonight, not between 'ere and our Polly up on Durward Street."

"Polly?"

"Oh, she's caught yer fancy then," said Nellie. "Well, I won't take offense. She's in need of a penny or two tonight."

And with that Nellie walked off, spying a more possible customer further down the road.

Once she was clearly out of sight, Llewellyn turned his face in the direction of Durward Street. It wasn't far, even though it meant passing the knacker's yard again. But no one gave him a second glance and soon he was walking alone in the silent gloom.

The road was dark and narrow. Grim buildings rose up around him; scowling windows glared at his passing but they did not stop him.

Unhindered he tapped his way along the cobbles, heading down its length to the corner where he knew he would find Polly. There was only one gaslight on this street and that was where the women would stand.

The monster within ignored Llewellyn's condemnations, the urgings to stop. He pushed the voice back. He had a task to perform and nothing would be allowed to prevent it. He could feel the weight of the axe and the knife inside his coat, could smell the blood on the apron beneath and it excited him. His hand found its way to the knife and curled around the handle.

This is it, Doctor, he murmured. *Can you stop me, this darkness inside you pushing to get out? You think it is Bercow who put me here. But did he? Who will truly be responsible for your actions? Watch me, Doctor, watch yourself. Be the observer in our little experiment.*

She was there. He could see her. The outline of her bonnet, proud in its shoddy defiance. She had not noticed him yet, not until he was upon her, towering over her slight frame. A monster that in other circumstances would have frightened her.

"'Ere, don't you go creeping up on a poor working girl." She laughed. "You out a'visitin' patients?"

Llewellyn said nothing, though God knows he tried, but the monster had silenced his voice. And in the end, it was this silence that stilled her chatter.

"Come on now, Doctor," she said. "You're preventin' me earnin' a penny."

"There are better ways," he said eventually.

"Such as?"

"Let me show you." He was grinning as he offered her his arm.

Polly leered back, complicit. She catered to all tastes. And he was a respectable sort. By now they had neared the stable-yard. He could imagine her pretending their silent promenade was one in which she pictured herself a genteel lady out with her beau. *A good joke*, he thought.

A flash of silver drew her eye. He saw her eyes widen as her brain registered what it was seeing but not soon enough to allow her to scream for help. With her mouth in a wide, silent 'O', the blade sliced through her neck; a second cut followed with such ferocity it almost severed her neck completely.

The parasite within allowed the true Llewellyn to look down at her, to wonder at how he managed such a deed, to be revolted at what he'd done, had become. This Llewellyn felt the creeping darkness that had taken hold of his heart, a pressure that was building up into a vice-like grip, a desperation as he sought to prevent himself from acting further.

But still he saw his hand cutting, slashing, ripping open her abdomen even as he fought to stay the blade. Something else was controlling him, something else was driving him on from inside— someone else. Isaac's voice. Lucy's voice. Genesis.

"You are cleaning the streets," said these myriad voices. *"You are ridding them of the corrupt, the foul, the immoral. You are the guardian of the poor, their protector. You must do your duty."*

His duty. Yes, this was his duty alright, his calling.

No, not him, not the man who was meant to heal, deliver relief. No!

But his protestations were answered by one of those voices from the darkness within.

"Oh yes, Doctor, you, and after all, are you still not delivering relief to those who suffer? As a man of science, you are duty bound to believe the evidence of your own eyes." And his protests were silenced as his parasite greedily continued to hunt the world from behind his eyes.

He could feel the bloodlust that drove the monster on.

Bloodlust, Doctor? Mine… or yours?

Llewellyn could sense the monster's need for release, for *more*, but already a grey light had begun to creep slowly through the miasma; it would soon be dawn. There was no time to act further, to test his skills against those of the slaughter men. That would have to be saved for another day, another victim.

Regretfully, *thankfully*, he pocketed his knives and strolled back towards Whitechapel Road. Nobody saw him and he saw nobody.

His own household was fast asleep and he was able to slip in unnoticed. It was an easy matter to hide his implements beneath the floorboards and change for bed. The parasite knew Llewellyn would often work late if he had been on a night call and bloodied clothes were not uncommon.

He felt he had barely closed his eyes when a commotion outside disturbed him. The banging sounded as though the door would be broken down at any minute.

He roused himself and made his way blearily down the stairs. An agitated PC Thain hovered nervously in the hallway. Llewellyn recognised the constable; their paths had often crossed as they went about their daily business. Both were well-known on the streets of the East End, although Llewellyn usually received a somewhat more welcoming reception.

"Beg your pardon to be calling so early," said Thain. "But we've a body down Buck's Row."

"Sorry, miss," he added, noticing Llewellyn's maid, Amy's, pale expression.

"Let me get my bag," replied the doctor, sighing. The spirit Llewellyn housed was still in the ascendant and it was he who would walk the streets. Despite his promise to Isaac about remaining in the night, he needed to retain control; there were bound to be awkward questions. He hovered on the edge of Llewellyn's consciousness, ready to step in at a moment's notice.

By now, Llewellyn's sister had joined them in the hallway.

"But my dear, you've not long got in. You must rest," she complained.

He smiled apologetically at her. "I will attend to this matter and then I promise I will take the day off."

She cast him a disbelieving look but said nothing.

He stepped out once more into the cold grey dawn, the adrenaline coursing through his veins helping to keep him awake. The two men walked quickly along streets that were slowly beginning to come to life with the approaching day. PC Thain carried a lantern, but it was of limited use in the fog that still enveloped them.

"You were out last night, sir?" asked the constable.

"Yes, an unfortunate case," Llewellyn said.

"Can I ask which part of Whitechapel?"

"Just off the main road, I believe. A young woman. She had suffered an assault of some sort, relatively minor for this area. I patched her up and sent her on her way."

"Our victim is a young woman," said Thain sadly.

"We live in dark times, Constable," said Llewellyn.

"We do indeed," replied the policeman.

They were near Durward Street. Just as they were about to turn into Buck's Row, a woman caught sight of them and dashed over.

"Oh, Doctor, Doctor," she sobbed. "It's 'er, it's our Polly."

"Come now, Nellie," said the doctor, trying to calm the woman. "Calm down and start again."

"It's Polly," she repeated.

The doctor looked at the constable with a shocked expression on his face.

The monster had said he would be caught. So soon though?

No, Doctor. Not yet, we still have a little more time together, you and I. Things to do, people to see. Let me deal with this little situation here. I can promise you it will be easy, oh so easy, for a respectable man like yourself to get away with murder.

Llewellyn shrank back from these words, lowered his eyes in what those around him regarded as a genuine expression of grief for one of his former patients.

"But that was the young woman I attended to," said his parasite, his voice suitably shocked and appalled.

"Yeah, you wos 'ere, last night, weren't you, Doctor?"

"Unfortunately, yes; even more unfortunately, I saw nothing."

"Now don't go blaming yourself, Dr Llewellyn."

The constable allowed him a minute to regain his composure and then led him to the gates of the stable-yard. It was darker here, the overhanging upper floors of the surrounding buildings casting a shadow over everything. So much of the business of Whitechapel was carried out in the dark.

There on the cobbles lay the body of Polly; the bonnet of which she had been so proud lay trampled nearby. She was on her back, her skirts tucked neatly around her.

The intruder inside faded away, allowed the real Llewellyn the stage but remained ever vigilant, ready to interfere should he be needed. This spirit had been cooped up in the minds of others for too long and did not relish losing his new home so soon. Despite his reluctance to relinquish control, this soul knew Llewellyn was often called out by the police for such examinations—the doctor knew the procedure whilst the intruder did not. He had to be clever.

"The constable"—Thain indicated PC Neil—"pulled her petticoats down to preserve her modesty. The dead should be treated with respect—whatever their background."

Llewellyn suppressed his annoyance. The constable was a decent man and his reaction was perfectly normal, but it prevented him getting a real picture of what had happened.

"Why do you need a picture, Doctor? You've seen it already." And the evil images that had been his reality that night returned in full force.

He moved closer to Polly to hide the turmoil that had taken control, took her lifeless hands, so cold now, and checked for a pulse he knew would not be there. He could see little in the gloom around him; the closeness of the surrounding buildings prevented any light entering, kept the approaching dawn well away from the dreadful sight. Thankfully it also kept any observers from noting the strange expression on his face.

The constable held the lantern closer to allow Llewellyn a better view. Oh, how clearly he could see the lacerations on her neck, the cuts he made, but the incisions, his little anatomical experimentations, those remained hidden.

Trying to suppress the images his parasite was forcing gloatingly forward, he quickly examined the rest of her body, noting how her legs, unlike her hands, still held some warmth. There seemed to be surprisingly little blood.

Of course. Are we not experts in our field? Now all you have to do is stay calm, whispered a voice from somewhere. *Don't give us away*.

Out of the corner of his eye, he could see Charley and Harry. *Don't look, don't give us away*, hissed the voice. Llewellyn couldn't recall them sighting him last night, but it was a risk even his normal self was not prepared to take. How could his life have taken such a horrible turn in such a short space of time?

How? You know how. And he remembered Isaac's laugh.

"You can take her to the mortuary now, Constable," he said to PC Thain. "The poor woman has not been dead beyond this half-hour, the cause obviously the cuts to her throat. Anything else will have to wait until I attend her at the mortuary to perform a more thorough examination."

Llewellyn could hear Charley and Harry giving an account of how they discovered the body, enjoying their minute in the limelight, conveniently forgetting they might be the next suspects to be considered. It would only take one voice in the crowd to call out a leading question and then others would follow. Harry might be gentle with four-legged beasts, but he was known to be useful with his fists, especially on his long-suffering wife—when he'd had a drink or two.

Nellie still stood at the edge of the crowd that had gathered despite the best efforts of PC Neil to disperse it.

Llewellyn wanted to turn away but was forced to look her directly in the eye. *You will attract suspicion,* whispered the voice in his head. *Let me speak.*

"I truly am sorry for the death of your friend," Llewellyn said. "If only she had allowed me to escort her home after I had tended to her, she might still be alive."

Nellie smiled at him sadly. "Yeah, Polly never was one for doin' the sensible thing, not when the thirst was drivin' 'er."

"I'm off home now, Constable," Llewellyn said to Thain. "It's been a long night and I need to rest. Let the inspector know I'll attend him at the mortuary this afternoon and I'll also make a statement. I'm sure you'll need one considering I was in the vicinity last night."

PC Thain tipped his hat respectfully. "Course, sir. It's all routine though. No one in their right minds would think for one second that you had anything to do with this."

The rest of the crowd murmured their agreement. Dr Llewellyn had treated and saved so many of them, he was their Guardian Angel.

He stopped long enough to watch them lift the corpse onto the back of a cart, an undignified and miserable end to an undignified and miserable life. The crowds parted, watching in silence as she was taken away, many knowing it could've been them, others knowing that one day it *would* be them.

The guilt ate at him, corroding everything he knew about himself as he walked slowly towards his home.

So, you have done what Bercow said you would do and what you claimed was impossible, said the voice in his head.

That wasn't me, protested Llewellyn feverishly as his tired eyes burned against the light.

No? Whose hand was it that cut and sliced and maimed? Whose hand touched the woman's flesh? Whose hand banished the light from her eyes?

That wasn't me, repeated Llewellyn.

Then who was it? Was it Bercow—no, scientific impossibility, or do you give him his due now? Or am I the dark shadow of you? Or am I simply the Devil? What do you believe, Doctor? What has the evidence of your own eyes told you during our midnight stroll?

Llewellyn pushed back the taunts but they remained there, continuing in their clamour, pushing him on and on, delighting in reminding him of their crime, torturing him with the desire to repeat the experience to cut, to cut, and cut…

He shook himself. *Think logically, think scientifically*, he told himself even as a voice laughed in the darkness. Yes, it had been a long night, that was all. Lack of sleep and the nature of his surroundings had combined to produce an unnatural melancholia within. Sleep was all he needed, sleep to get rid of that strange voice. Sleep and a good breakfast.

Yet when he reached his house, he found he could not go in. To go back into that innocent household was tantamount to desecration.

He looked up at his house. A solid, reliable presence in the uncertainty of the East End, much as he himself had come to be viewed. Now all that was slipping away.

Amy had spotted him from the window and stood with the door open, ready. He stared at her and then without knowing why, or where he was going, he turned and walked away.

"Sir," she called after him. "Sir."

But he ignored her and kept walking. Only when he stopped did he recognise his destination. He was at Isaac's house. Would his friend be able to penetrate this cloud that was fogging his mind?

You still think of him as your friend, Doctor?

He knocked on the door and Dominic answered.

Llewellyn tried to push past him but Dominic's bulk prevented him.

The voice in his head laughed at Llewellyn's feebleness. He could join in, make it easy for the Doctor, but sometimes he just liked to sit on the sidelines and watch. It made for good entertainment and added to the doubt his host felt about his own sanity.

Llewellyn backtracked. "Could you tell Dr Bercow I apologise for the unholy hour, but I need to see him. It's… it's urgent."

The servant said nothing, merely inclined his head and directed Llewellyn to the parlour. A fire had already been made up, as if Isaac were expecting company despite the time.

A maid entered and placed a pot of coffee at his side. What was her name? Ah yes, Susanna or something. He watched her go. Isaac had such amenable servants. Quiet, unobtrusive, biddable. He wished his own household was the same. Amy always seemed to be watching him. So did his sister.

Perhaps… murmured the voice.

A sudden image of their lifeless bodies rose in his mind; his cup clattered back onto its saucer, coffee spilling across the tray.

No, no!

But once seen, those images could not be unseen. And they were few among many others.

His invader started whispering again, mocking tones that froze Llewellyn's heart, his soul.

Oh, come now, Doctor. Have you forgotten so soon? We both got to know Susanna pretty well, not so long ago. You think she's amenable. Oh yes, she was amenable alright. And you enjoyed yourself so thoroughly, so… methodically. That's how I would describe you, Doctor. Methodical.

He pushed the voice away, tried to focus on his own life, the normality of it all, his own maid.

Ah, dear little Amy, delicious little Amy.

His sister had teased Llewellyn she was sweet on him; totally inappropriate of course. He hoped that was the reason for her attention and not that she suspected something. Either way, he would have to take steps, find her another position. Regardless of her feelings, she was making him uncomfortable in his own home.

He stared into the fire, allowing the dancing flames to soothe his tormented thoughts, wishing he could stay there and just not be troubled any more.

Why send her away when we could find something more enjoyable to do together?

Eventually the door opened and Isaac entered. He did not seem surprised to see Llewellyn.

"Under normal circumstances I would apologise for this unearthly hour," said Llewellyn, getting to his feet. "But considering the nature of events and your… part in it …" He could not finish.

"Please, please compose yourself," said Isaac directing Llewellyn back to his chair. "The hour is not that early."

Isaac checked his silver watch as he spoke, a normal action allowing the appearance of the tool of his trade to appear naturally, to start swinging, to catch the light of the fire and dazzle the doctor's eyes.

"Rest, my dear Llewellyn," he said as the chain swung back and forth. "You have had a long night and are tired. Rest, you are safe here."

The words sounded false to Llewellyn's ears but even so his eyes betrayed him and followed the chain, back and forth, back and forth.

"Such an easy subject," murmured Bercow.

Slowly Llewellyn's consciousness deserted him, but his eyes didn't close. From the darkness came another, came the voice that occupied so much of his mind, his thoughts, and, ever more, his actions.

"Are you there?" said Isaac.

"*Where else would I be?*" mocked the parasite.

"My instructions were for you to leave the good doctor out of your activities."

"*How do you know I didn't?*"

"From the fact that he is currently in my parlour right now and obviously in a disturbed frame of mind."

"*You were the one who instructed me. It was you who directed me to kill, you who sent his conscience into the dark whilst I walked; you created me in him. We share the same mind, but you have built a very thin wall between our realms.*"

Memories of his own occupation, the pushing at the boundaries of his own mind, came rushing back, the thought that somehow they could break through, the fear of the result. What would happen if the barrier he had built between Llewellyn and intruder were to come down? Who would emerge the victor? Llewellyn had accused him of playing dangerous games with people's minds, but Isaac didn't play games. This was his experiment.

And if the doctor was to be kept safe to act his part, then he had to allow this spirit more freedom. His cunning was needed in the daylight hours as well as the dark. Without it the man would get caught and would hang. For a crime he didn't knowingly commit.

Isaac thought back to his earlier conversation with Llewellyn. Was the evil that had been wrought, the murder, really his doing or was it a part of Llewellyn he had never seen before? That inner darkness lurking hidden beneath the depths of the beating heart, unseen by anyone, unheard, except maybe as a little voice that sometimes found small relief in a strong word or slammed door when really, truly, they wanted to do more?

His study of hypnotherapy was taking him down strange paths. Had the spirit been a figment of his own imagination which he planted into Llewellyn's thoughts as a suggestion, or had he been truly the dispossessed soul gifted by Genesis into his safe keeping until he could home him, or worse, was he himself mad?

He could *not* begin to doubt himself now, too much was at stake.

He looked at Llewellyn, saw the shadow looking out from behind the doctor's eyes, and knew it was too late to go back. There was nothing to be done except see the experiment through, but there were a few steps he could take to assuage his conscience.

"You will be ever present," he said, as if he had any choice in the matter. "But it will be with my friend's safety uppermost in your mind at all times. I gave him to you on that understanding. And when I bring him back you will be—gentle with him."

"*Why not just bury him completely?*" asked the parasite.

They both knew this was a charade. Isaac was in control of nothing, but he could try.

"No," said Isaac. Llewellyn annoyed him in many ways, but the man did not deserve that. "You need his knowledge, his skills. You must develop a way of working together."

He swung his chain and slowly, very slowly, in the silence of his parlour he brought Llewellyn back.

The doctor stared at Isaac with utter horror on his face.

Isaac knew what he was feeling, what dark memories were being thrown up to him from the night before. Llewellyn was fully aware of everything; nothing had been held back.

"What… did… you *do* to me? What did you *do*?"

The man looked distraught. His eyes wild, shining with terror.

"My dear fellow—" Isaac held his arms out in a gesture of supplication.

"You've played those damned tricks of yours on me, haven't you?"

"What do you mean?" asked Isaac, keeping his face deliberately void of expression.

"I hear a voice, in here." Llewellyn tapped his head. "He… he tells me we have done… things. He has shown me memories in my own head of which I have no knowledge. He has shown me in the despicable act of murder. *Me,* a doctor who has sworn a sacred oath to protect human life. *Me*—" He was choking now, barely able to get the words out.

"You sneered at my theories," said Isaac. "You said it was all trickery, quackery, mere illusion. So tell me, if it is no more than a showman's flummery, how can you hold me to account for your own actions? Couldn't it be that you've merely let your true self out?"

"You believe that I have always held such evil in my heart?" asked Llewellyn. "No, never. It must be you, it can't be me, it can't—"

"Yes," said Isaac, leaning forward, waiting for Llewellyn's capitulation. That was all he wanted, that recognition.

Llewellyn let out an unearthly groan and buried his face in his hands. The man's body shook with sobs, rocking back overwhelmed at what had been inflicted upon him and what he had done to others.

Isaac observed him dispassionately. Sometimes you had to bury your emotions in order to retain control of the situation. A lesson Llewellyn, too, would have to learn.

"Do you agree then I have some skill, a genuine control over the consciousness of others?"

Llewellyn stared hard at Isaac as if he could not believe the man were demanding validation of his methods given the circumstances. But if he denied him, then it meant the monster was something borne within himself, something he had procreated and brought to the light. Bercow knew he would get the answer he sought, and then the man would grovel if he had to, beg Bercow to put an end to it.

"This… thing, this voice in my head," said Llewellyn. "Will it stop? Can you make it stop?"

Isaac turned away from the doctor. There was no way he could make it stop. To do that meant he would have to go back on his promise to Genesis and that was something Genesis would never allow to happen.

Where was Genesis? Was he watching, listening to the lies being told?

Perhaps in time he would be able to find a solution, he usually did, thought Isaac. He had Llewellyn believing in him now. But what would Llewellyn do?

Bercow can do nothing, said the darkness to Llewellyn. *He has no power over you... or me. He thinks I am an experiment but in truth I am merely a wandering soul who has been given a home by a power stronger than any he can call upon.*

At that, Llewellyn came out of himself. "At least I am in the clear for that poor girl's killing. I suppose I must thank you."

"It was your other self's quick thinking that protected you."

"And his murderous activities that endangered me in the first place," said Llewellyn. Then he stood up, composing his features, the stern Victorian once more.

"I will go about my business as usual," he said. "But from this point on I consider our friendship at an end. I… I will deal with this *thing*, this other self, and there will be no more murders, no more deceit. And I will make sure that you *never* rise above your current station."

That stung—both Isaac and the shadow. How *dare* he? Did he still assume he had any control over his current situation?

"You forget, Doctor, I know everything," Isaac said coldly. "I could let the authorities in on your nasty little secret."

But it was not Llewellyn who replied; another was determined to show who had the upper hand out of all of them. *"And you forget, Isaac,"* said Llewellyn's other voice. *"He has me and I will think for both of us."*

And then Isaac knew war had been declared. He could see the doctor looking at him in terror as Llewellyn realised that after all this, after the words he had just spoken, there was no hope. He went to take out his watch but Llewellyn's hand stayed him.

"No, Dr Bercow. I know all your little tricks. I will not allow you any more control over me. No one will ever control me again. Together the doctor and I will cast the blackest of stains across society."

"And what does Doctor Llewellyn have to say about that?" asked Isaac.

"He doesn't. He's being very sensible and staying quiet."

Isaac shuddered as the man slammed out of the house. There was no doubt now as to who held the upper hand in that relationship, despite Llewellyn's earlier brave words.

It should be easy to let him go, forget about Llewellyn, just let the monster that occupied him do as he would, one less nuisance to have to consider but no, the doctor would have to be watched, just in case his own name was raised in discussion. He needed to know what the man—although which one he wasn't sure—got up to.

He wouldn't put it past Llewellyn to implicate him in the recent murder. It wasn't that he was a stranger to such a crime, he, too, carried a darker stain than most, but he would not be called to account for something for which he was not responsible, conveniently forgetting he was the one who had started it all.

Now, though, was not the time to dwell on theories nor on past actions. He had to be practical. If need be, he could arrange for a little accident. The streets of Whitechapel, as had been proved last night, were not very safe.

He summoned Dominic.

"Follow him," said Isaac. "And if you can't, hire someone who can. The doctor isn't… isn't well."

Dominic simply nodded. The instruction wasn't an unusual one; his role as Isaac's assistant often led him out onto the street, a place which had once been his home.

Isaac looked out the window. Llewellyn had vanished around the corner, but the bulky figure of Dominic was not far behind in pursuit.

Isaac would not allow Llewellyn to ruin his plans; he was a mere hiccup in his grand scheme. He reached for his notes and turned his thoughts back to Lucy. That predicted a more pleasant, and more profitable, future. She was the key to so many minds, and he intended to unlock all the possibilities.

"Vanity," whispered Genesis, "all is vanity."

But Isaac did not hear him.

Chapter Five

Llewellyn rushed out of the house not knowing which way to go. Too many thoughts crowded his mind, pushed to be heard. Unable to differentiate between his own inner voice and that… that trespasser inflicted upon him by Isaac, he closed himself down, fixed his eye on the road ahead and walked.

He counted every step, using the logical regularity, the certainty of numbers, to repel the invading whisperings. The rhythm gave him comfort, soothed him with its certainty.

One, two, three, four…

"'Ere guv, mind where you're goin'."

The jolt to his arm disoriented him slightly, sent him feeling automatically for his pocketbook, a habit born of years spent amongst the pickpockets and thieves in the East End. He glared down at the boy, a street urchin, filthy and ragged, a young body with an old man's eyes. He was looking at the doctor strangely and he must have seen something that scared him for he started to back away.

"Sorry, s-s-sorry, mister." The boy cast him one more wary look and then sprinted off into the night.

Five, six, seven, eight, nine, ten…

"'Ello, dearie, give a girl a penny? She'll warm your 'eart and other parts besides."

The woman accosted him as he passed the Flowers. She lurked at the entrance to an alley nearby, no doubt the scene for all her tawdry alliances, convenient for both picking up customers and for spending her earnings. The dirt cloaked her, too, caked into her dress and into her soul.

She looked up at him with bloodshot eyes; he could smell the spirits on her breath, the other men. Disgust and revulsion rose up from within him. And again, this woman also saw something that caused her to retreat quickly from him.

Eleven, twelve, thirteen… fifty-one, fifty-two.

He passed an inn, would've given anything to be sat in the warmth amongst friendly faces, nursing a small brandy, but kept walking. It wouldn't do to suddenly start talking aloud with no visible companion.

He wandered the street aimlessly for a while, keeping to the shadows as so many did at that hour. Those that he passed tended to avert their eyes; not seeing was standard practise, a survival technique learnt from an early age, even more important in the light of recent events.

The mist closed in around him, shifting as figures loomed up briefly and were then swallowed again. He pulled the brim of his hat further over his eyes and turned the collar of his coat up. He could hear voices shouting, a brief burst of laughter, a blaze of light and then silence and darkness once more as his feet took him down the alleys and towards the docks.

Focus on the numbers, seventy-one, seventy-two, seventy-three...

On and on through the dark of the night, on and on with so much humanity around him but occupying a completely separate world to the one he now inhabited. He felt isolated, utterly alone.

The creeping, snagging fog becoming denser with every step meant the river was nearby, a murky blanket that swirled and twisted its cold, damp fingers around him, claiming him, marking him as its own. He pulled his collar further up, tried to prevent those probing tendrils from invading him any further but still he could feel the creep of ice through his pores, into his blood, slowing him down.

One hundred, one hundred and one, one hundred and two...

He stamped his feet harder as he walked, trying to prevent the numbness that had begun to attack him from the cobbles, their hard, rigid surface rising up without warning in an attempt to halt his progress, trip him up. His flight had become a stumble.

He passed another tap room. The group of men gathered outside looked curiously at him as he passed. They probably thought him worse-for-wear, just another drunk.

He crashed on, aware only of the hammering of his heart, the protest of his lungs, footsteps... *footsteps*. These were more than his own, their weight and pace sounded like a man, more than one man.

He broke himself from his trance and looked back. Saw four shadowy figures hiding in the walls. It was the group of men he had just passed. They obviously considered him an easy target.

He stopped and waited. Why, he would not have able to tell you, only that he had no intention of running, that too many people seemed to be telling him what to do. Perhaps he thought there was an honesty in the approach of these four ruffians; he knew what their intent, their purpose, was, and he welcomed it.

Reckon we could both do with a little exercise; blow the cobwebs away, came the whisper.

"No!"

Llewellyn lashed out with his fist as if to punch the invader but instead he found his knuckles make satisfying contact with one of the followers who had peeled themselves away from the walls. The man staggered back under the force of the blow, obviously surprised by the strength of the man they considered easy prey.

Another burly figure launched itself at him. Anger boiled up inside Llewellyn, fury at the way he'd been treated, despair at what the future had in store; it roiled away, stoking itself into a rage so red he was almost blinded by its intensity. He allowed his body to feed off this energy, garnering its strength for himself, using it to vent his frustrations on his assailants. He heard nothing, not his own voice, not the whisper, just the howl of his own rage which he let out into the night.

Two men came for him, one trying to grab his arms and pin him back, but again Llewellyn fought them off. Nothing could stop him; nothing could beat him in this madness which claimed him. He punched and clawed, a snarling menace that looked at his attackers with a merciless eye. There was blood, and it felt good. He wanted more.

Go on, more, more…

The whisper. He struck out again, trying to lose himself in the rage of the fight, submerge himself in the pain of the blows, release himself from this unwanted presence. And so he fought until the men crawled, stumbled off into the darkness, leaving only one poor soul lying at his feet too stunned to move.

Llewellyn looked down at him without pity, transferred all his misery into a final blow, and then walked away. He did not check to see whether the man was dead or alive. He felt no concern, only a euphoria as the adrenaline continued to surge through his body. Nobody would report him; it would have meant revealing their own criminal intent.

He started to count again, but this time held his head higher, his back straighter. He still felt strong, invincible. And it felt good.

One, two, three…

He looked about him. Started to take in his surroundings, his fellow travellers of the night. Cold, cold, cold but the warmth of his anger, its embers still flickering, sustained him against this continual attack.

Twenty-one, twenty-two, twenty-three…

The rhythm soothed him, relaxed him further. He knew where he was. Through numerous little alleys he caught glimpses of moving lamps briefly illuminating the ghostly outlines of a sail here, a hull there, a warehouse window.

His walk had brought him back towards life. The hour was late but the streets were filling, slaughterers finishing their work, stevedores and dockers toiling, grim shapes distorted by the flame into crook-backed monsters.

He turned down one of the alleys, not afraid of what it might hide. It was only a short walk to the dockside. He felt invincible. He stopped counting, opened his ears to the voices around him while still ignoring the one he knew was waiting, biding his time before they would finally confront one another… again.

He passed a broken door, a window whose shutter did not hide the hovel that lurked behind it. A small fire puckered in the grate and men, despondent, weary, sat around, barely able to talk. A woman turned at the sound of his steps, stepped quickly out as if to accost him, the promise of a good time. He walked on, not even acknowledging her. She watched him go, curiosity evident, then shrugged her shoulders and returned inside. There would be others, there would always be others.

Glimpses of misery accompanied that short walk but still he felt his own situation far outweighed the trials he saw. He stepped out of the narrow street unscathed and strangely refreshed.

Yea, though I have walked through the Valley of Death ...

Soon he would listen but not just yet.

Shadwell Dock loomed up ahead of him. Huge warehouses towered over everything, lit up brightly enough to make you think it was almost daylight. It defied the mist, sending it back to the Thames so you could only see it if you moved back towards the darkness.

Llewellyn straightened himself up further, flexed his fingers from the claw they had settled into after the fight, breathed deeply, and walked on. A group of burly men were loading barrels onto a cart, swearing cheerfully at each other in a language he did not recognise. Another group sang a bawdy song, language and sentiments all unfortunately too evident. They ignored him.

So many of life's outcasts ended up working these docks. It was hard work, labour that did not demand a degree, an intelligence, just brute physicality. No questions were asked so even the lowest criminal could get a job here should he so choose. Here would be a home should he ever need one.

There was a crash as a huge chain was allowed to drop to the ground to be swiftly coiled and moved back to the workshops for whatever repairs were needed, a giant metal serpent that coiled and writhed before it allowed itself to be tamed by the boys who fought to get it under control.

They dragged it towards open doors from where a furnace blazed, delivering their victim to the Devil's kitchen. The flames briefly illuminated the boys' faces, blackened and strained but with eyes shining brightly. So far, their labour had not dimmed their spirits, a state of affairs that would surely not last for much longer.

Above his head, a maze of catwalks ran between the buildings and little figures ran to and fro; so much purpose in their life, so busy, and all just to earn enough for a loaf of bread.

His walk took him towards Shadwell Stairs, the women were waiting there as he knew they were in such places all along the Thames. Whenever the ships were in, they would gather, flocking towards these parts as surely as carrion crows hover over the dead; both picking their victims clean.

He strode by, stepping over a drunk sprawled across his path, who just as surely ignored Llewellyn. An empty gin bottle rolled out of his hand. Other shapes lay on the ground, curled up against the night, sleeping as soundly as if they were in a normal bed, and for them, they were.

Further he went, until he took a path leading towards the river, narrow and untamed; weeds and bramble clambered over the muck and filth, showing how little used this track was. He looked around and could see no one. Only when he let out a deep breath did he realise how tightly he had been holding himself.

It was time to find out who or what this intruder really was, time to let him speak. He offered up a silent prayer.

No point in that, Doctor. No one there to hear you. God gave up on us long ago. You only have to look around us.

Llewellyn groaned aloud.

Don't despair, Doctor. This could be the start of a mutually beneficial relationship.

"In what possible way?"

You want to know how I got here, how Isaac Bercow created me?

"Yes."

And I would assume you would want to know how to rid yourself of me?

"Yes."

Then know this. I know all of Bercow's secrets, his little tricks, his experiments, his… failings.

"And what would you expect in return?"

I need my amusements, my… entertainments, and of course you would have to help me find a new home.

"These amusements of yours, these needs. Are they in the same vein as the murder of that poor girl?"

That was not murder. I have made a study of anatomy—which makes us a perfect partnership—and I have further experiments to make. You must not stop me. If you do, you will find you will lose your mind forever and I will be in control.

"And how am I to know that you won't try and take over anyway?"

You won't.

Llewellyn didn't just hear his voice. He felt his presence, a shape, an entity, walking the neural pathways of his mind, reading his history, finding out his darkest secrets, his deepest hopes.

Nothing that comprised his essence was sacred to him anymore. He was an open book.

A consultation with Bercow came back to him. It had taken place a year or two back when they had been discussing one of Llewellyn's patients who had begun to suffer nervous fits on a regular basis. Careful questioning had revealed an incident of a delicate nature which upset her greatly; remembering it caused these fits.

Llewellyn had brought his patient to Bercow, and the doctor had taught her a trick. He told her to imagine a big chest and to picture herself placing that memory in the box. She was then instructed to close the chest and lock it, throwing away the key.

It took a little while for the visualisation to work; sometimes the box had a habit of flying open at the most inopportune time and she would have a fit, but eventually it remained closed and she no longer suffered.

Could he create a safe place in his own mind to protect his thoughts and ideas, or better still, a cell in which to lock the intruder?

You could try but I doubt you would succeed. A little challenge for the two of us? Perhaps we should place bets.

The mocking laughter rolled around his head, bringing back with it that feeling of pressure, claustrophobic and intense.

Don't worry, Doctor. I won't spend too much time talking to you. It wouldn't do for you to have a nervous breakdown before I complete my research. I will give you space to think, to breathe, to live, but I will know everything.

And then he disappeared, not completely, no, that was too much to hope for, but he faded sufficiently into the background so he was the mere hint of a presence hovering in the wings.

Llewellyn accepted the silence with relief, staring into the dark waters of the Thames below him as it lapped the shores below. The deep, deep stillness beneath the surface looked peaceful; he imagined himself wrapped up, submerged in that inky blackness. So tempting.

No... not yet.

During this one-sided conversation, a figure lurked in the shadows. Dominic had been able to follow the doctor despite the labyrinth into which he dived. He had been surprised at the doctor's ability to throw off his earlier assailants and then watched nonplussed as the doctor talked to himself.

Perhaps Isaac had played one of his little tricks on the man, thought Dominic. He could not bring himself to disapprove. The doctor always appeared to look down on them whenever he came to the house. Reckoned he was too good for them. But there was something about this new doctor, the one who fought in the dark, that he admired.

Dominic decided to watch him a little more closely, and not just because Isaac had demanded it.

Chapter Six

Lucy. She was a puzzle Isaac still had to resolve. He had passed off her presence as the recently discovered niece of a brother long-forgotten, left behind in the dark corners of his childhood. It was an acceptable answer. Charity begins at home was a motto oft repeated in the drawing rooms of society.

He'd grown used to her presence but never really talked to her about where she came from or how she came to know Genesis. He'd asked a few questions when she first arrived, but she ignored them and eventually he gave up.

Perhaps it was about time he discovered a little more about his partner, considering she was increasingly going to be sharing the stage with him. He could not afford any embarrassing incidents.

Dominic was out again, following Llewellyn as directed whilst Mary and Susanna were preparing themselves for the evening's performance. It would be some time before they returned.

Lucy was sat on her stool as usual. Funny how she preferred this plain seat to the more comfortable chairs in the room.

"Not really," she answered. "I prefer the solidity of something from the natural world. Wood is a beautiful material, is it not?"

It was going to be one of those conversations, he thought. Should anyone observe them now, they would appear just silent two figures, a subject fit for those sentimental paintings so beloved of society. He doubted they would see any fatherly expression on his face and the girl would certainly not exhibit any aspect of filial duty. How would anyone read them?

"An interesting question," she replied. "But it is not one which concerns us. I doubt anyone will ever paint our portraits."

That shook him slightly. One of his dearest dreams was of one day inviting guests into his house, into his drawing room where they would admire his taste in furniture, art, his portrait on the wall…

"And now you want to know if I've hinted at something darker in your future." She smiled.

And the smile was her answer. Cold and ancient, she was the crone who dragged you to hell.

"No," she said. "No need to drag you. You walked all the way here on your own."

Isaac forced himself to concentrate on what he wanted to ask, dismissed her ominous comments. "Where are you from?"

She frowned at that. "Everywhere."

"Pardon?"

"I am made up from the lives of millions who lived like me. Creatures forced to crawl in the gutter, feed on the filth and waste."

"How can that be? You are flesh and bone," he said.

"Aah, but do I bleed?" And she held out her hand to him.

He realised then that in all this time he had never actually touched her. She took his hand firmly, her grip an unforgiving vice. There was no softness, no suggestion of heat below, and when she moved his hand to her wrist he could detect no pulse.

"You thought me a corpse when we first met."

He swallowed, dreading the revelation she was about to make.

"Don't worry. I am no corpse."

Isaac felt some small relief at that. It did not last long.

"I am no corpse because I am not human. I take your form but that is so I can move freely amongst you. And I am only one of many. There are others of us. All servants of Genesis. The conduits for his plans, his energies. We exist at all levels, in the gutter, in the drawing rooms of the great and the good, in church and chapel. We are everywhere. We are legion."

"Genesis," he whispered. "Who is he?"

She laughed. Her mouth widening, wider, wider, threatening to engulf him its terrible void. And when she spoke, it was no longer her voice. Instead, he heard the cry of thousands, a cacophony that assaulted him, drowning out every awareness of where he was, who he was. Slowly the cries merged until they became one, became Genesis. "Do you understand who I am now?" he asked.

And Isaac understood. He'd refused to believe in anything beyond the world around him. Denied the existence of both God and Devil. He had been wrong.

"You were born in my fires," Genesis told Isaac. "You were raised in my training grounds. You were mine from the first."

Despair was something Isaac had never fully experienced before. All his life he'd risen above the knocks and the hardship, driven to be something more than the creature he'd been born, determined to prove he was not his father's son.

"Oh, but you are. You have proved that time and time again. As I said, you were mine from the first."

"No."

"Your father chose my path long ago," said Genesis. "It was only fitting any child of his would also be mine."

"No."

"The wickedness of your mother only added to your purity, your capacity for evil. She promised me her only begotten son many years ago."

"No."

"And so I am denied three times." Genesis laughed. "How very appropriate. But I will not take it personally. We still have much work to do, you and I. You will help me spread the seeds of chaos."

"And if I don't?"

"There is only one other choice you have. One that would bring you into my company that much sooner. I do not believe that that is a path you wish to follow."

The world was spinning out of control and Isaac felt as if he must fall at any moment; a fall that would take him to the very pits of Hell.

"No," said Genesis, his voice softer, calmer. "That is not for you—if you do as I bid. I will ensure that you have the life you wish for as long as you wish, provided you obey me."

Isaac sat down carefully. Tried to steady himself, bring some rationality back into this world turned upside down. His head began to pound and he knew the parasites within him were moving forward. They had been watching and listening to this interchange and now they decided it was their turn to speak.

They told him of the things they had done and the lives they had led under the guidance of Genesis. Of his ability to give them whatever they desired, whatever the cost, if they served well.

And their voices grew. A swell that became louder and louder until he could take no more and collapsed back in his chair... oblivious to everything around him.

Lucy smiled and returned to her stool. Then her gaze became vacant once more.

When Susanna and Mary returned, that was how they were found.

"There is time yet before the performance," said Dominic, entering quietly behind them. "Why don't we have a drink to get ourselves warmed up?"

The three removed themselves to the kitchen.

Lucy continued to smile and her smile sent its stain over her surroundings, into the threadbare carpet, into the sagging cushions and mildewed curtains, into the world Isaac could never leave behind even though he might try. And Lucy intended to let him try.

You should always give a man hope, for a little while, she mused.

Chapter Seven

From behind the heavy drapes, Isaac watched Mrs Wintringham's servants busy themselves. Lamps and candles blazed across the room, their light catching the crystal glasses and decanters adorning the sideboards.

He listened to the soft rustle of the maids' dresses as they went about their business, adding the last touches before the guests entered, a melodious chink and glint of glass and silver.

Rows of highly polished mahogany chairs were arranged in a semi-circle around his own central position. The intimacy of this setting provided no scope for any of his normal tricks. Everybody would be able to see everything, and perhaps that was for the best. Nobody could accuse him of being a fraud.

As the guests arrived, the music changed to the sound of silk and velvet, and he inhaled lavender and rose water instead of sweat and filth. But he knew this was just a mask; strip it away and the men and women were just like the audiences at the music hall. There was still dirt underneath, but it was a better class of dirt and even better, it was paying dirt.

He was thinking too much. Losing focus. That wasn't good. His head still felt heavy from his earlier interview with Genesis, but it was a small audience; he should be able to get through the evening.

"*Don't worry*," whispered the voices who had not shuffled back into the darkness as expected, as he had hoped. "*We are with you.*"

Isaac pulled himself up straight. He could not let on that anything was wrong. He had come too far to let anything destroy this chance. He may have done a deal with the Devil, but he was still a showman. He would deliver.

"I know you will," murmured Lucy, but he knew it was Genesis speaking.

And what an audience he had; Mrs Wintringham had outdone herself. Finally, she had delivered him his entry into society proper.

Lucy was also there but she remained carefully hidden behind the curtains. They had agreed she would communicate with him in her usual manner, but he would take centre stage that night. She would observe, then she would help Isaac develop the act he hoped would finally lead to his acceptance into the Royal Society.

Genesis had plans for that illustrious body; to control science via the realms of somewhere—the power of someone—they denied was too delicious an irony to resist. Tonight was a testing ground to see what sort of response Isaac would receive from his so-called betters, to see if Genesis had chosen well.

Isaac glanced at Lucy. She was quieter than she had ever been. He wondered that she had so little to say after the events of the day.

"You have others to speak with you and for you tonight," she said. "It's best I give them room to function. They can be very creative."

Her response did little to reassure him, but she promised to step in from time to time. He was grateful for that, and at least her appearance had much improved. She was clean, modest, the deathly pallor gone—just in case someone saw her. There were standards that had to be kept up in public.

He knew Genesis would also be watching through Lucy's eyes. An uncomfortable thought but only to be expected. Checking his progress both in public and in private.

Well, he'd delivered on one front already. Llewellyn was out and about, a vehicle for one of Genesis' unanchored souls, his *brothers*. He should approve of that at least.

With difficulty, Isaac pulled his thoughts back from Genesis Caul to the scene in front of him.

The room was brightly lit for the present. Candles and oil lamps cast merry shadows around the walls, welcoming those who entered. Here were Honourables, Lords and Ladies even. They would demand gentle treatment, sympathy and understanding, not the gaudy show necessary for the costers.

He would also have to be respectful, both of their position and their learning; he could not afford to overreach himself here in case they declared him a charlatan. Tonight, he would have to swallow his pride somewhat—and hold his tongue.

"*Why?*" whispered the voices. "*We can do anything.*"

The room was almost full and an air of expectation hovered over those present. The eyes of the women sparkled with excitement whilst the men maintained a more aloof appearance, but even amongst them there were one or two who were obviously keen to see what would happen.

"Doctor Bercow." Mary's voice broke into his thoughts. She always addressed him thus in public; it added to their apparent respectability.

Someone somewhere was laughing in the darkness. He wiped his brow with his kerchief.

Mary was looking at him and tapping her pocket watch impatiently. It was time. He sighed heavily; he would be glad when such shows became a thing of the past. The lights had gone down, and the audience stilled its murmurings and fan-fluttering. He felt he could almost reach out and touch the air of expectancy that hovered over them.

Dominic had only just returned after setting up a new watch on Llewellyn. So far, the doctor continued to go about his daily routines in his normal manner; only occasionally did whoever was trailing him report back that he seemed to spend a lot of time talking to himself when he was on his own. Either way, nothing untoward had happened and Isaac felt he could push that particular matter to the back of his mind for the moment.

All his concentration, all his effort, was needed for tonight, not just to maintain his own self-control but also to direct and manage his little team, particularly Dominic. One wrong slip, one careless word, and all his plans could come crashing down.

A single lamp illuminated Dominic, his usual master of ceremonies and sometimes partner in crime, an association that had lasted for a good twenty years. He had to admit, time was beginning to take its toll on both of them; the man was visibly sweating under the glare of the light, a sign he he'd been drinking despite his promise to Isaac.

Never a small man, Dominic's girth had increased considerably as he had begun to enjoy the rewards of their improving fortunes; unfortunately, his sense of taste had not adapted to their new position despite Isaac's best efforts. In short, Dominic had begun to look seedy and down-at-heel, not the impression Isaac wanted his show to give. Luckily, they would not have to do many more once he'd put his little project into action. And then he would retire Dominic.

"*He can be ours*," said the voices.

Isaac took a last look in the mirror. Flecks of grey were beginning to encroach on his once jet-black hair, but he'd decided to let it be; there would be no boot-blacking for him. Silver gave out a distinguished, more venerable air that encouraged others to approach him more willingly. Women in particular seemed to find the look attractive. His brown eyes were now mercifully clear of their earlier bloodshot look.

He faked a smile. He looked the epitome of respectability, of calm self-assurance. Tomorrow, Mrs Wintringham's guests would be discussing the evening's events in their own parlours, spreading his name even further afield. As was the nature of women, he had no doubt his appearance and marital status would be dissected and discussed in detail.

He adjusted his shirt collar and smoothed down his jacket. He looked ready. He *was* ready. Tonight, he would make them believe.

We will make them believe.

Isaac took his place at the side of the small dais that had been raised as a makeshift stage. This was an intimate gathering after all, not some music hall performance.

Dominic was almost finished with his introduction. Mary had taken up her place on one side of the parlour, Susanna on the other. He looked towards Mary. She discreetly nodded her head. He did the same to Susanna. Both were dressed as members of the audience, their gowns hired especially for the occasion.

They were set. He wondered if the women were aware at all this would probably be one of their last performances, although he was going to give them a grand finale of their own. Centre stage.

A voice refocused his attention back to the present.

"Coming to terms with loss," Dominic was saying, "is one of the hardest things we have to deal with. The times of loneliness and despair, the overwhelming grief, all this brings a sense of isolation and unbearable pain. Yet it does not have to be this way. Your loved ones are never far from you. They may have left this world, but they have not abandoned you. They *are* nearby." He paused for a minute, allowing his silence to spread out across the auditorium.

"They are here," he continued, deliberately quieting his voice, giving his words a certainty they knew would send shivers down the spine.

"Tonight, you are privileged to have with you the renowned doctor and spiritualist, Isaac Bercow. He has come to you to lift the veil between the spirit world and our own earthly realm. He will put you in touch with your loved ones. He will bring you comfort. He will help you heal." Another pause. "Ladies and Gentlemen. I give you... Doctor Isaac Bercow."

The glow of a light spread to reveal Isaac and followed him as he moved to centre stage. Dominic had already disappeared into the wings.

Isaac perched himself on a high stool and quietly surveyed his audience once more. Very slowly he took in all their faces, allowing himself to make eye contact with some. These would be the ones he would pick. They were the ones who glowed in their desperation.

As he paused, he knew that Dominic and his assistants would be taking note of those he lingered over and would be swiftly looking up their notes, reviewing their codes. His act was finely honed; by ensuring the focus on himself, they never noticed any subterfuge going on around them.

In truth he no longer had need of his assistants, but he had decided to carry on in the old way for the time being, regardless of the help he received from those in his head or from Lucy. He could not dismiss them outright, they knew too much.

When he finished his initial surveillance, he walked to the edge of the stage and held out his arms in an all-embracing gesture.

"Welcome," he said. "Welcome to you all, for whatever reason you have come. Many of you will be here to seek comfort, to hear from your loved ones, perhaps to make peace... with them and with yourselves. I will bring the spirits to you; I will let them talk. Even now, I can sense them, waiting in the shadows."

He paused and scanned the room again, heightening the expectancy even further. "It is no longer quiet in their world," he said. "The veil is lifting and they are coming through. They are now among us. They are with us."

With satisfaction he could see eyes flicking nervously from side to side, trying to conceal both their curiosity and their excitement from their neighbours. The lights around the edge of the room were dimmed.

"I hear whispering," he said. "But there is one voice, louder than the others. A child. A girl."

He waited. There had been one or two gasps. Some muffled sobs. He would have to tread carefully. Isaac did not regard himself as a fraud. He saw what he did as fulfilling a need, providing a service. Still, when it involved a child caution was necessary; personally, he never understood the attachment. His own upbringing had been devoid of all sentiment, the purpose of children as far his father was concerned was for the money they would bring in to the family from whatever line of work the parent deemed fit.

Nor did he receive much in the way of maternal affection; he and his siblings were merely a drain on their mother's energy, on her purse, too many mouths to feed, too much noise. Their neighbours had been the same and when children decided it was preferable to flee and try their luck independently than to stay at home, their parents never tried to stop them, indeed rarely acknowledged they'd gone. No one ever seemed to ask after them and the authorities certainly didn't seem to care.

How different in these gentrified circles. How they mollycoddled and pampered their offspring with their nurseries and nannies, their eagerness to display the accomplishments of their child whose sole purpose was to marry rather than be of any direct use to society. And, oh, how they looked down on anyone who dared do an honest day's work—not that Isaac could boast of that either.

He kept any speech brief, simple, reassuring. Such tactics ensured his reputation. He put a hand to his ear as if he were listening to someone.

"She says her name is Mary? No... wait... Marianne. Does anybody know a Marianne?"

A woman nervously raised her hand.

"You recognised the name, madam?" asked Isaac.

The woman nodded and fixed her eyes on his. "My... my daughter was called Marianne," she said.

"She's young," said Isaac before turning his face away from the audience as if in conversation with someone at his shoulder. "What?" he asked. "You're how old? Five? Six? Oh, seven."

"Marianne," cried the woman, half-rising from her chair, one hand clutching the armrest.

"Marianne says you've been worrying about her for too long. She says that she's fine, that she's with, she's with, who?"

Again, he turned his face from the audience. Lucy was talking to him.

"Leonard and Grace?"

"My parents," whispered the woman. "She's with her grandparents."

A smile had appeared on her face. He had her. *Thank you, Lucy. My pleasure.*

"They say hello too. They say that they're looking after her. There's no need for you to be sad anymore. Let her go."

"But it's so hard, she was so little..."

"You have other children, they say. Concentrate on them."

She stared at him for a moment, a struggle clearly going on inside her head. Then finally it was as if the fight had gone out of her and she gave a small little nod. The man in the dress suit at her side took her hand, an expression of relief evident on his face.

Lord and Lady Fullerton. They had been amongst the first to accept the invitations from Mrs Wintringham to his little soirée. Isaac's informants had provided him with a fairly detailed description of the family, including Lord Fullerton's increasing despair at his wife's inability to put the death of their youngest child behind them and to give the remaining children, and himself, the love and support they deserved.

For a moment, Lady Fullerton looked as though she were going to speak again, he needed to move on. It didn't do to get into too long a conversation with audience members. The more it went on, the greater the risk of making a mistake.

Oh, we wouldn't let you do that.

He pretended to hear another voice. He would do this his way for as long as he could, until he had handed the other members of his little troupe over to Genesis. Another payment in kind.

Nice to know you haven't completely forgotten our little arrangement.

How could he with those voices in his head, their clamours for freedom in the dead of night when the world slept but he was condemned to toss and turn?

"Richard. I have Richard here," he continued. "Does this name mean anything to anybody?"

A number of people stirred in their seats and looked around. Richard was a very common name.

"Richard tells me that he died overseas. Some sort of expedition?"

"Damned fool," growled an elderly man from beneath heavy eyebrows. The woman seated next to him gave a visible dig in the ribs with her fan.

"Richard was our eldest son," she explained. "He went to America, invested in a gold mine out there."

"Idiot wasn't content with just investing though," said her husband. "Oh no, he had to go down the damned mine itself. Look where it got him."

Another dig in the ribs.

"You'll excuse my husband, Doctor Bercow. We had high hopes of Richard taking over the family business and now..." She trailed off.

"And now we're stuck with his idiot younger brother as well," finished her husband.

Isaac smiled to himself. The idiot younger brother had become a regular drinking partner of his in recent months. It had not been difficult to discover the financial difficulties in which he found himself, and which he had not revealed to his father for obvious reasons. They had concocted a scheme which would not only solve Matthew's problems but also provide them with a little windfall.

"You do understand that I run a reputable show," he'd said to Matthew. "To pretend in any way is a terrible betrayal of the trust of my audience."

"This would be a one-off," assured Matthew. "The money will be mine by rights when he dies anyway. I just get some of it that little bit sooner."

Isaac agreed to Matthew's request albeit with apparent considerable reluctance. He also had to make sure he had some security in case Matthew should ever try to undermine him in public. Susanna had taken care of that.

"Richard says you're to trust your other son. He says that giving him more financial independence will make him more responsible."

"Give him money? Are you mad?"

Sir Stephen's wife gave him a hard slap with the fan. He glared at her but said nothing. Arguing in public wasn't the done thing.

"He really thinks that will help?" she asked.

"Richard says yes and that as you've tried everything else, what could you possibly have to lose?"

"Just the family fortune," muttered Sir Stephen.

"Now, dear. It's not as though we'd give him everything, just enough to set him up. He's an adult now, after all. And if we set him up with a young wife..."

There was a small spluttering sound behind the curtains which thankfully the audience could not hear. Isaac smiled to himself. Matthew would have to sort out the marital issue on his own; Isaac had stuck to his side of the bargain, had got him his money. In a few days, Isaac would be able to cash the cheque Matthew had already written out.

"*He's mine*," said a voice.

"*Later*," said the others.

There were two more conversations between the living and the seemingly dead and then Isaac had the welcome relief of a short interval. He declined the sherry and port that was on offer—a clear head was vital on such evenings—but gladly accepted a cup of tea.

A number of guests offered him their cards, expressing interest in holding a similar soirée in their own homes; he tucked these into his pocket but did not enter into any prolonged conversations. They always asked him questions about his life, and he did not want to give anything away. He made his way through the small crowd and returned to Lucy's side.

"An impressive show," she said.

"And it will be even better next time. Then, I will bring you onto the stage. Show the world what we are capable of."

He returned to the drawing room. A fan tapped his arm. Mrs Wintringham. He needed to keep her hooked, for now.

"You know that you will need to book another appointment with me? It will take several consultations before you are completely cured."

She nodded girlishly, a slight flush spreading over her cheek. Isaac found that it helped when his patients fell a little in love with him. He looked around.

He could see this evening's patron, Sir David Threlfal, on the other side of the room. An industrial magnate. Self-made man. Cynic. Isaac knew Sir David would be trying to catch him out, looking for some way to trip him up. It was Sir David's fiancée who wanted to see Isaac's 'act', and as she was an heiress of extensive means, Sir David had to agree.

"I must thank you for speaking to Sir David for me."

Isaac and Dominic had spent a considerable amount of time and effort discovering everything they could about both the Threlfal family and that of Sir David's fiancée. They had to be prepared.

Mrs Wintringham continued to flutter around him in an irritating way; a nod to Mary and she came over and manoeuvred the silly old bag away. It wouldn't do to have her eavesdropping on their conversation. Now Sir David was coming over to them. *Pompous fool*, thought Isaac, but he fixed a subservient smile on his face.

"Sir David!" he said. "I must say this has proved to an exceptionally successful evening."

"*Humph*," said Sir David dismissively. "Lot of old hokum if you ask me. And I still think meddling with the mind is unnatural, dangerous, even though Mrs Wintringham here begs to differ. You won't mind though, Doctor Bercow, if I choose to remain somewhat sceptical over the matter?"

"Not at all, Sir David. Everyone is entitled to their opinion. Perhaps you would like to sit in as an observer one day?"

"Perhaps," said Sir David and moved away to resume his seat. He had done his duty as a host and been polite to the man. He didn't need to speak to Bercow anymore.

The rest of the gathering took their cue from him and also returned to their seats. This was the signal for the second half of the show. Isaac was more than satisfied; Sir David's cynicism would ensure his attendance at one of Isaac's consultations.

Then one of the monsters that roamed inside his head could have him. The thought was a pleasing one.

The spirits were very talkative for the rest of that evening. Lord Pomfrey spoke to the brother that disappeared in the Himalayas. Lady Carlton made peace with her mother. The Right Hon. Felix Stavebury discovered his kinship to the FitzGeralds of Sussex—a fortuitous link that allowed him a claim on the estate of the recently deceased Marmaduke FitzGerald who died without heirs.

When the evening was finally over, Isaac had a lot of satisfied customers and the offer of a number of future bookings. Dominic gave him a nod from the hall doorway. It meant he'd received their payment for the night and, from the grin on his face, there was also a considerable bonus.

"Doctor Bercow."

Isaac turned to find Lady Elizabeth Moreton at his elbow, the soon-to-be Elizabeth Threlfal. She was young, and he had to admit, very beautiful. He wondered what on earth attracted her to a man like Sir David? She seemed happy enough about the projected marriage. *Probably just doing her filial duty and following Papa's orders.*

"Lady Moreton! I must thank you again for inviting me here. I hope you found the evening informative?"

"Informative and enjoyable, Doctor Bercow. You have made a number of my friends very happy." Her clear blue eyes sparkled up at him,

If only she knew.

"I am glad, Lady Moreton. I feel I have a responsibility to use my gift for the comfort of others."

"Well, you have certainly achieved that. Goodnight, Doctor Bercow. I hope we will meet again."

"*So do we,*" murmured the voices. There now seemed to be some considerable argument going on his head as to which of them was to claim Sir David and in consequence, Lady Moreton. He pushed their unsavoury imaginings into the background.

Isaac bowed low over her hand. "I hope we will too. Goodnight."

He followed Dominic out to their waiting cab. It looked small and insignificant compared to the carriages of the others, but it was sufficient. He felt it best to appear modest and humble amongst such people. They were more inclined to offer their patronage if he represented no threat. Besides, Isaac needed to conserve his money for the time being.

He waited before most of the other carriages had gone before commanding the driver to move off, pausing around the corner to pick up Mary and Susanna. The two women climbed in giggling and rosy-cheeked, whether from the cold night air or the small flask of gin that Mary was holding he wasn't sure. He would have to watch these two; drunkenness loosened tongues.

Lucy had already disappeared as she usually did at night. The others barely realised she had gone. So far, she had not taken centre stage, so they paid her little attention, regarded her as just another of Isaac's pet projects. Whatever she did or said had so far failed to make much impression upon them.

"So, are we going to celebrate?" asked Susanna, snuggling up to Dominic. He pushed her away, just as he always did. Isaac smiled. Dominic was not what you would call a ladies' man.

"I think we can allow ourselves a *small* something at the lodging house," said Isaac.

"You have a plan?" asked the voices, knowing full well his intentions.

Susanna glared at him. Isaac knew that wasn't what she had in mind.

"Look, this is the start of something big—for *all* of us. We can't afford to make any mistakes right now."

He turned and looked out the window. It was yet another cold and foggy night. The cab made its way through the narrow streets of Whitechapel, an area which meant Isaac had to pay double the rate if he wanted to get home. One day he would show this place a clean pair of heels.

He watched the shadows loom and merge in the swirling mist, occasionally making out a figure beneath an isolated gaslight. On nights such as this there were still people out working the street despite the danger that threatened them. The need for money or drink or both drove them on in their desperation.

"Glad I'm not working this patch anymore," said Mary, shivering as she looked out on the same scene.

"And I hope you will never have to again," said Isaac. Both Mary and Susanna glanced at him sharply. They understood the threat that was buried beneath this sentiment. Life had become less risky and more comfortable, provided they did as they were told.

The fear and unease rife in the East End had spread beyond its boundaries and lapped insistently at the doors of the better-off. The deaths attributed to Saucy Jack had still not been solved, but since that initial killing spree there had been no further murders—well, no more than was usual—but this did little to dispel the general feeling that lawlessness reigned.

It meant people looked for answers and reassurances wherever they could. It meant business was good for Isaac. Good, but he wanted better; he also wanted to settle an old score.

He had come a long way from the gutter, and it had been a hard climb. It would, however, be a quick and easy fall should things go wrong.

"We won't let that happen."

They neared the local Workers Institute. Outside, a man stood holding a placard proclaiming the End of Days. It was late but the doom mongers worked twenty-four hours a day looking for souls to save. This particular gentleman had a good position, behind him the Institute, in front of him the Lord Nelson.

The cab pulled up and its occupants disembarked, the women pulling their cloaks tighter around their shoulders, pointedly turning their backs on the public house. That establishment had been an old stomping ground of theirs, and among its customers there were still bound to be one or two who remembered them. They did not want to be reminded about what they had been.

"We should move lodgings," said Mary, as she did every time they returned.

Isaac looked at her, a slight smile on his face. "It never does to forget where you came from."

"You think we can ever forget?" asked Susanna with a shudder. "The memories are never far away."

"We will move," said Isaac. "Just not yet. Soon we will all have enough money to set ourselves up like proper gentry. You'll be able to choose where you live then."

Dominic had been silent until that point.

"You haven't yet explained exactly what you have mind," he said. "Don't you think it's about time?"

"You're right. It is time. Let's get inside, warm ourselves up, and I'll explain everything. I can guarantee you'll like my idea."

He hadn't meant to carry out this part of his plan so early on in the game, but the opportunity had presented itself and later on, well, they might be more suspicious.

Tonight, they were tired but content; their guards would be down. Open minds, unguarded, trusting, were the most susceptible. His companions were not completely naive, they had survived many years on these harsh streets, but they trusted him.

"Evening, Harry," he said to the doom monger as they walked past. "Convinced anyone this evening?"

"Nah, managed to relieve them of some of their more earthly worries, though." He grinned as he said this and patted his pocket.

Discussions about the end of the world made for easy pickings, especially from those who had been to the tavern.

Isaac smiled and turned into the alleyway at the side of the Institute. He strode purposefully along in the dark, ignoring the rank puddles in which he occasionally stepped but remaining alert to figures that might be hiding in the shadows. Those who haunted this particular byway had learnt long ago to leave Isaac alone. He'd shown a skill with a knife that would have done credit to the Ripper.

Occasionally, rumours reached his ears that some considered he was in fact the infamous murderer. He found it amusing but did nothing to dissuade people of their opinions. If they feared him, then all well and good.

"Why do we have to go this way all the time?" complained Susanna as she trod in something indescribable.

"Throw people off our trail," said Dominic as he opened the door to their dwelling.

"Is someone on our trail then?" asked Mary.

"No," said Dominic. "But it doesn't hurt to take precautions."

Mary moved swiftly around the room, lighting the lamps and bringing a soft, homely glow to their surroundings. Susanna lit the stove and set to work heating up the remains of their earlier meal. One of Isaac's doctrines was to waste nothing and they had learnt quickly. Dominic lit the fire in the hearth.

Isaac, meanwhile, took up his seat in the armchair by the fire and nursed the glass of port Mary had brought to him. He allowed himself one drink only as a reward for the evening's work.

It was always tempting to take another drink, but he'd been down that road before and he did not intend to travel that way again. This drink was, in a way, a test of his own willpower.

Dominic, by contrast, had a bottle of gin at his side and was already pouring out a second glass for himself. Isaac had intended to talk to him about his drinking. Tonight though, a slightly inebriated Dominic would serve his purpose. He would let the women indulge as well. He fetched another bottle of gin from the cupboard and poured two glasses out.

"Mary, Susanna," he called. The two women came through from the kitchen, slightly surprised looks on their faces as he offered them the glasses. "A little reward for your hard work this evening," he said. "Come, sit down."

The four sat quietly around the fireplace enjoying the peace and satisfaction of a good evening's work. Isaac allowed them to sit like this for some time, refilling their glasses until he felt they were sufficiently relaxed for his work to begin.

"We've had a good long run with our spirit friends," he said. "People take us seriously now, but I think it's time for us to move on and develop new avenues of income. My name is known and trusted and that will serve us well for what I propose."

He looked round at his companions, who nodded their agreement. Their faces were flushed from both the warmth and the alcohol. Their bodies were completely relaxed. Their eyes were focussed on him.

"You know that I have recently been treating patients who exhibit signs of nervous hysteria and anxiety. The method I have used involves hypnosis; it allows me to rewire their minds, so to speak, so that whatever fears or psychosis they have are removed as my instructions speak to their subconsciousness."

They all nodded again but he doubted they fully understood the implications of what he had been saying. They had no scientific training and did not read the journals he brought back to the lodging.

Nor had they attended his clinic in Waverley Road. They didn't even know it existed. He merely told them he'd be treating his patients in their own homes. He had, however, rented respectable premises to conduct his appointments and that was where much of their recent takings had been going. They had accepted his explanation that he'd been investing money for them, which was true in a way.

Chapter Eight

Isaac felt a pressure behind his eyes. The others were back, watching, jostling for position. Now he had released one of them, the others were vying to be the next to experience freedom. Perhaps he could kill two birds with one stone? But how would he prevent them from knowing every detail of his plans?

"Too late for that, Isaac," said one. *"But we are prepared to accept what you will give. You seem to have a flair for mayhem. Even a short space of time will allow us to indulge our tastes."*

A roar of laughter. Then a growing chant of *"let us out, let us out, let us out…"*

"And I can always bring them back," said Genesis.

"My hypnotherapy," said Isaac, turning his attention to his earthly companions, "allows me to put my subject into a trance-like state. Once they are in that condition, they are not aware of anything going on around them, they are only aware of me, they only obey me."

Dominic gave a cynical chuckle. "If that is the case, why aren't more people doing it? If you can control people, you can control their money. We'd never have to work again."

"And that is exactly what I am planning," said Isaac, his face serious.

"You can really control people in this way?" asked Mary, doubtfully.

"Yes, and I have already done so. You notice Elizabeth Moreton attended this evening's soirée. I have recently started her on a course of hypnotherapy and to test how far I could control her at the present I instructed her she *had* to attend. And she came."

Mary still looked doubtful. "How do you know it was your hypnosis? The girl's infatuated with you regardless of her engagement; she'd have gone to the ends of the earth if you'd asked, engagement or no."

Susanna nodded her agreement.

"Well perhaps I could give you a little demonstration now if you want," he said.

The three looked at him warily.

"Don't worry," he said, making sure he sounded reassuring. "I won't get you doing anything ridiculous, not like those music hall acts where they get you stood up clucking like chickens or biting heads off rats."

"You promise?" asked Susanna.

"Yes, and when did I ever go back on a promise?"

The three looked at each other and then at him.

"Alright," said Dominic. "Who's to be hypnotised?"

Isaac looked directly at him. "You," he said. He knew Dominic was the least suggestible, the most suspicious. He would be able to put the women under much more easily. He took out his silver pocket watch. It gleamed in the firelight.

"The first step to getting a person into a trance is to get them to focus on something and ignore everything else around them. I always use my watch."

He moved his chair nearer to Dominic so he was sat directly in front of him. He indicated to Susanna and Mary to move in closer so they could study his technique.

"I want all of you to focus on my watch. As I swing it back and forth, I want you to think of nothing else. Let your mind empty; breathe steadily."

He started to swing the watch chain. Dominic seemed to fight it at first and then, with his eyes, gradually submitted to the pull of the chain. Out of the corner of his eye, Isaac could see both Mary and Susanna were also entering the same state.

He had never thought to hypnotise more than one person at a time, but when Elizabeth had attended her last session, the maid that accompanied her had also gone into a trance-like state. That had got him thinking.

"There is nothing else around you," he said softly. "You are warm, you are comfortable, you are safe."

He continued to swing the chain. Dominic's eyelids started to droop, the women likewise. "You are happy, you trust me. Your eyelids are growing heavy; you must rest them. Let them close. Let them rest. *Rest*."

Dominic closed his eyes. The women did the same. Isaac stopped swinging the watch. They made no movement, no sound. He looked steadily at each of them but they did not move. He returned the watch to his pocket.

"*Very impressive*," said the voices.

They could be playacting, Isaac thought, but he had a test ready.

"Mary," he said, "show me your locket."

Obediently she pulled her necklace out from under her blouse.

"Open it and show me the picture."

She did as she was told, revealing an image of herself and a young girl. Whilst she always obeyed Isaac, the one thing she always refused to do was reveal to him the contents of that locket.

"Who is the girl?"

"My sister," she said.

"What happened to her?"

"I killed her." There was no emotion in her voice, nothing on her face to convey the gravity of her words.

He looked sharply at her. Her revelation was completely unexpected.

"How did you kill her?" Woman as murderer. He knew it happened. Had come across such creatures from time to time, but it was still a rarity.

"She tried to steal my food. I pushed her. She fell down the stairs. I hid her body in the yard."

"Nobody searched for her, nobody discovered her?"

"No. Ma was grateful to have one less mouth to feed and kids running away was common enough. As to the smell, well our place smelt bad all the time anyway. She made no difference."

Isaac had to admit he was shocked. He did not expect emotion under hypnosis unless he suggested it, but her monotone voice and flat delivery was unnerving—particularly as she showed no sign of such psychosis under normal circumstances. He wondered what secrets the others held but there was no time for that. An induced trance like this one would not last very long. He had to work quickly.

"Sleep now, Mary. Send the world away for just a while. I will call you back when needed."

The woman's head slumped forward onto her breast. Her chest rose and fell gently; a silvery trail of saliva ran from the corner of her open mouth.

Isaac turned his attention to Dominic. Did he feel regretful at the steps he was about to take? Perhaps, just a little. The man had been useful, served a purpose, but now Isaac had no more need of him. Except to provide a little bit more evidence supporting his initial theory about the black stain residing in all humans.

What could he really make this hulk of a man do? How far could he push him? He knew Dominic was capable of killing, had in fact murdered on more than one occasion, usually at Isaac's instruction but in a fully conscious state of mind. What Isaac was going to ask him to do now was on a completely different level. Would his subconscious provide any resistance to the instructions he was now going to give? There was only one way to find out.

"Dominic," he said. "Can you hear me?"

"Yes." The man sat rigid in his chair, his bulk straining against the shabby finery of his clothing.

"You are my partner, aren't you?" Isaac had always held the upper hand in their relationship but often referred to Dominic as his partner, a subtle flattery that paid off on many occasions when there was dirty work to be done.

"Yes." A slight smile, a hint of pride.

"We need to get rid of the women. They are taking too much of our profit. You do agree, don't you? Tell me, Dominic, what we must do."

Dominic nodded, appearing to consider Isaac's words. "We must get rid of the women," he repeated. There was no sign of perplexity, though, no hint of concern over his agreed betrayal of his friends.

"There is no time to waste. You must do it soon." Isaac had become impatient to put the penny gaffs behind him. "When will you rid us of these women?"

"Soon."

Isaac found such complete acceptance of his instructions satisfying, exhilarating even. "Tomorrow you will dispose of Mary and Susanna," he continued. "Tell me what you will do tomorrow?"

"I will get rid of the women."

And Isaac described how Dominic would do this, how even their deaths were to be a performance, a tribute to the theatrical way of life the small troupe was leaving behind. But then there was that one last command. "Once you have completed this task, I have one final instruction for you, Dominic. Do you understand?"

Dominic nodded his head.

"My friend," said Isaac, "once the women are dead, then you must kill yourself."

There was no flicker of surprise on Dominic's face, no gasp of shock from Mary and Susanna; the two women still appeared fast asleep.

"Dominic," said Isaac. "Did you hear me?"

"Yes."

"Tell me what I have asked you to do, what you *must* do after you have disposed of the women."

"Kill myself." Just like that. Complete, unutterable acceptance.

Isaac smiled. It was all so easy. He heard a round of applause in his head. Another little problem neatly tied up, another link to his past broken. He felt no qualms, no pang of guilt; people like themselves just did what had to be done.

Isaac picked up his watch again and held it up in front of Dominic. "All three of you will open your eyes and focus on my watch."

Three pairs of eyes opened and regarded the watch with apparent interest.

"The watch made you tired, so I am going to put it away. As I lower my hand the watch will disappear from your view. I will count slowly to five. As I count you will start to feel wakeful. When I reach five you will return to consciousness."

He started to lower the watch. "One... two... three... four... FIVE!"

The three were immediately alert.

Dominic looked at him. "When's this hypnosis meant to start then?" he asked.

Isaac laughed. "I've already done it," he said.

His companions looked shocked. They patted themselves discreetly to see if anything had been taken or changed.

"Don't worry," he said. "I didn't do anything to you. What sort of friend would I be if I did something like that?"

"How do we know you hypnotised us?" asked Mary.

"I asked *you* to do something."

"Me? What did I do?"

"You showed me your locket."

Mary's hand went to swiftly to her throat, feeling for the reassuring presence of the chain. She pulled it out from beneath her blouse and watched the silver glint in the reflection of the fire.

"I asked you to open it," he continued.

"I would never do that," she whispered.

"So you say," he replied. "But you did. You showed me the photograph."

"I don't believe you."

"It's a picture of you and your sister; you told me what happened."

Mary gasped in shock. "No," she whispered. "No."

"I'm afraid you did. Shall we discuss what you did?"

Mary looked at Dominic and Susanna who were both regarding her curiously.

"No," she whispered again. "No. I believe you."

The other two didn't look completely convinced but that was no matter. He had set his plan into action. They could all just relax and enjoy the evening together as usual.

Isaac set up the card table and brought more gin and port out. Dominic grinned. He always thought he could beat Isaac at cards but for some reason he never did, nor could he stop rising to the challenge. Strange that. Tonight, though, he felt his luck was in.

"Come on, ladies," he said, getting up and walking slightly unsteadily to his place. Mary and Suzanna followed, giggling as they tripped over their skirts. Isaac noticed that beneath the laughter Mary still had a slightly distressed look on her face. Perhaps he could let her win a hand or two as a distraction. The money would be coming back to him soon anyway.

The rest of the evening passed pleasantly. Mary won and soon perked up. Dominic still lost but he did it with good enough humour. Isaac sat back in his chair and regarded his companions. It was a shame this was to be the last evening they spent in each other's company. Still, needs must when the Devil drives, as his old pa used to say.

His father. He had not thought about him for many years now. His last sight of him had been of him hanging from the end of a rope, his feet twitching in their death dance.

Those around him had urged him to run forward and pull down on his legs to quicken his end but Isaac had refused. His companions put it down to shock; he was only a young boy after all. What they didn't know was that Isaac wanted to see him dance. His father had been condemned to eternal suffering and he wanted to make sure that he suffered one last time in this life before he burned in Hell.

Despite the passage of time, Isaac involuntarily raised his hand to his neck and rubbed at it as if it were sore. More than once his father had tried to strangle him in one of his drunken rages. Perhaps that was why he enjoyed watching his father's last public performance so much.

That was about the only thing we had in common, he thought. *Putting on a performance.* Come tomorrow, though, he would become a greater murderer than his father had ever been. Of that he was certain. He felt no shame about it, no guilt, it just felt perfectly natural.

He recalled the evolutionary theories of Spencer and Darwin. In the debate on natural selection, it was Spencer who coined the term 'survival of the fittest.' A phrase that felt suitably appropriate to his current circumstances. He was putting evolutionary theory into practise—and you couldn't argue with science.

He woke to the smell of something burning. That meant it was Susanna's turn to cook the breakfast. Still, he only had to endure her cremated offerings one more time. He thought of his other rooms above his clinic. Far more comfortable than here. He looked forward to being able to leave all this behind him. Isaac was taking another step up the ladder.

He dressed quickly; the early winter was already making its presence felt and the cold was seeping up through the floorboards. He would shave later, he decided. His remaining clothes were already packed in a carpet bag under the bed. There was very little left to do to ensure a quick departure.

Dominic and Mary were already sat at the small table, valiantly trying to eat what Susanna had put in front of them. He smiled sympathetically at them before sitting down and joining them. This was their last meal together.

"Any plans for today?" he asked Dominic.

Dominic chewed thoughtfully. "You wanted a bit more information on the Moreton family, didn't you?"

Isaac thought quickly. It was true he needed to know as much as he could about the Moretons, but he did not want the others near that family if his little plan was going to be carried out today. Their names would be directly linked to him and then he would never get near Lady Elizabeth again.

"Yes, but it can wait a while."

Dominic raised his eyebrows. Isaac had done nothing but push them hard in their search for anything and everything about the Moretons and the Threlfals. A few skeletons were rattling in their cupboards.

Isaac smiled. "We had a good night last night. I think we could all do with a day off; it is so rare we get such a chance. I already have an engagement, but why don't you three go and enjoy yourselves? Perhaps the music hall?"

He put a small purse on the table. "I think you'll find there's sufficient in there for a show and supper."

Mary and Susanna grinned happily at each other. Dominic looked slightly dazed. Isaac had said the trigger words. Now there would be no going back.

"Dom. Dominic," said Mary. "Are you alright?"

"Hm? Oh, yes, yes."

Isaac pushed the remains of his breakfast away. It was time to take his leave of them. He glanced at his pocket watch.

"If you'll excuse me, I must be off. I have arranged to meet with Lady Carlton."

"A booking?"

"Perhaps. I think she would be a prime candidate for hypnotherapy. I have it on good authority she suffers from stomach pains on a regular basis but so far nobody has been able to ascertain their cause."

He put on his heavy coat and wrapped a scarf around his face before picking up his hat.

"You look a right toff!" exclaimed Susanna, laughing.

"Anything for my clients," he said, suppressing his annoyance. Her comment hadn't been much, but it reminded him he was not yet what he wanted to be. The others seemed happy in their current station. They had a security they'd never known and enough money to get some little enjoyment out of life. That wasn't enough for Isaac.

He opened the door and cast a last look back at them. His companions were all smiling at him, happy at the good fortune they were experiencing. He gave a small nod and left, stepping out into the bitter cold air of a January morning. Patches of ice covered the pavements; mud and sludge had hardened into lethal ridges. He trod carefully as he made his way down Gregson Street, giving a brief *good morning* to the vendors that he passed.

He paused when young Tommy Jones passed by. The boy was a good informer and could be a ghost when needed.

"Hey," he called.

Tommy stopped and looked across at him. Doctor Bercow meant money. He wasn't disappointed. He pocketed the coins Isaac gave him and ran off. Elizabeth wouldn't even know he was there. One day, one day soon, she would acknowledge Isaac publicly.

He continued on his way. The streets slowly became more respectable and occasional hansom cabs passed him by. He would flag one down but not yet. He needed to get further away.

He wrapped his scarf tighter around his face, obscuring his features as he did so. There was nothing unusual in this; it was perfectly natural in such cold weather. He thrust his hands deeper in his pocket and strode on.

Finally, he felt it was safe enough to flag down a cab to take him to Waverly Road.

He dismounted to the pavement and looked around him with satisfaction. This was where he belonged. Soon he would never have to go back to the Rookeries again.

The door opened before he even had a chance to knock. Emily bobbed a curtsey.

"Good morning, sir," she said. "I've been looking out for you. There's a fire in the parlour if you'd like to go through and I'll have cook bring you up something to eat."

He smiled down at the girl. A pretty little thing. She came with good references. He passed her his hat and coat.

Lucy was already perched on her stool by the fire.

Back at the lodging rooms, the three had finished what passed for their breakfast and were bickering amiably about how to spend the day.

"Lord Nelson?" teased Susanna.

Mary shook her head. "Never again," she said resolutely, remembering the king of all hangovers she had suffered as a result of her last visit.

"Pleasure Gardens?" she suggested.

"Bit early for that isn't it, ladies... and I use the term loosely," said Dominic.

"What's wrong with you?" asked Mary. "Bear with a sore head this morning."

"Missing his boyfriend," said Susanna maliciously.

Dominic started to raise his hand but thought better of it.

"I don't feel quite right," he said. "Probably going down with something."

The women became a bit more sympathetic then.

"Fresh air is what we need," said Mary. "A stroll down by the river, then we can walk up past the music hall, see who's on, maybe have a spot of lunch."

"That's it," said Dominic with sudden decision. "Getting out and about will make me feel much better."

They wrapped themselves up in their coats and mufflers and locked the rooms behind them. Stepping out into the street, they linked arms, Dominic in the middle, the women on either side. He towered over them. Nobody ever threatened them when Dominic was around. Mary and Susanna felt safe in his company.

Their walk took them round the busy streets of the docks where initial looks of interest at the women were swiftly replaced with an unsure glance at Dominic and then a return to work. They kept up a reasonable pace—it was too cold to amble—but already Dominic felt his head clearing.

The Black Eagle Music Hall was looming up ahead of them as their circuit took them back to the busy byways of Whitechapel. It was closed, as he expected it would be at that time. The evening's entertainment was listed on weather-beaten poster.

King Salamander was topping the bill tonight. A fire-eating act that both Mary and Susanna had heard of and wanted to see for themselves. Seeing the words calmed him; his earlier vagueness had gone.

"That's this evening settled then," he said, and the women clapped their hands in delight.

Isaac had just finished his breakfast—porridge, devilled kidneys, a marked contrast to Susanna's well-meant, but poor, earlier offering. He sat back with a contented sigh and picked up the morning paper.

An announcement in the public notices informed him of the date of the coming nuptials of Sir David Threlfal and Lady Elizabeth. An invitation would be nice, he mused; he would have to see about getting one. The social pages were tiresome in their triviality but he read them assiduously. He had to make sure he made no social gaffes as he rose through the ranks.

He glanced at the clock on the mantelpiece. Almost eleven o'clock. Lady Carlton would be here shortly. He rang the bell for Emily who came and quickly cleared away his breakfast things.

"Make sure we have some suitable refreshment ready for Lady Carlton," he reminded her.

Perhaps some smelling salts, he thought sourly; she was sure to have an attack of the vapours. If anyone mentioned nerves to her, an attack could almost always be guaranteed to happen. She probably spent hours in front of the bedroom mirror practising her 'natural' swoon.

He did not think there was any truth in her affliction. Like so many women with no real purpose in their lives, they invented a condition that guaranteed them attention and sympathy and also ensured an excuse to sit around all day doing nothing. She would, he knew, be susceptible to his suggestions.

The wheels of a carriage pulled up outside. He resisted the urge to go to the window and look out. Part of his appeal was his aloofness. To be seen as too eager, too keen, was death to a reputation.

Emily's soft footsteps passed by the doorway and he heard her open the door and greet Lady Carlton with the right amount of deference. He had spent some time coaching her in social etiquette and now she was playing her part to perfection.

In time, he would have to take on a butler. That would be a more appropriate servant to have in place. Emily would not object, especially if she was given the title of housekeeper. Perhaps it was time to put up his prices. The more expensive you were, the more people wanted to come and see you. The aristocracy were such snobs.

The door opened and Emily announced Lady Carlton.

"Ah, my dear Lady Carlton," said Isaac walking over to greet her, taking her small gloved hand in his and bowing low. He retained a gentle hold of her arm and led her to her chair. He took his seat opposite her and leaned forward, concern etched in every line of his face.

"Dr Bercow," said Lady Carlton. "It was *so* good of you to agree to see me at such short notice."

"Not at all, Lady Carlton. I do not like to see people in distress, and I was most concerned last night when I saw you suffer so grievously after dinner."

She'd stuffed her face with truffles; beef, pâté, trifle, every delicacy that had been on offer, she'd tried it. Her suffering was indigestion brought on by her own greed. She knew that, he knew that, but neither of them was going to mention it. They both currently had a role to play.

"You're very kind," she said. "I felt better after some rest; however I still feel slightly under the weather."

Her flesh was straining hard against her clothing. Her corset alone was probably cutting off her air supply. He shuddered as an uncalled-for picture of her in her corset suddenly appeared unbidden in his mind. He hoped she wouldn't ask him to examine her. No matter how much she irritated him, and even repulsed him, he needed her... for the present.

"You told me last night someone recommended me, but we were interrupted. Would you mind telling me who?"

"Why, of course. It was young Elizabeth Moreton, and I must say she is looking so much better these days. Positively blooming. In fact, I would hazard a guess and say she has a beau hidden away."

He noticed that she was looking keenly at him.

"Now, now, Lady Carlton," he replied in an equally teasing manner. "Young girls and their infatuations are not to my taste. I prefer the more mature woman. I find they are much pleasanter and more agreeable company."

His flattering comments hit their mark as Lady Carlton blushed slightly and took a sip of her tea to hide her momentary discomposure.

"Although I cannot discuss the specifics of Elizabeth's condition with you—I am sure you appreciate client confidentiality, I can say that she has responded extremely well to my course of hypnotherapy. You may have heard of this?"

"I have seen some reports in the paper," she replied. "I believe the Society is giving a lecture tonight; my husband has decided to go."

Isaac pricked up his ears. He had tickets to that evening's lecture but had debated whether or not to go. So many reports accused practitioners of hypnosis as charlatans that he felt by presenting himself on a more public stage he would be condemned and dismissed before he even got started. The newspapers delighted in listing the names of those who attended such functions.

"He heard Professor Sorenson is speaking. He has always held the scientific opinion of this man in high regard."

That was good news. Sorenson was a strong advocate of the use of hypnosis in the field of medicine. If Lord Carlton approved of Sorenson, he would surely be more inclined to support his wife and so give Bercow the opportunity of demonstrating his skills.

His treatment of Mrs Wintringham was beginning to pay off in more ways than one. He would go to the Society lecture. It would also keep him away from any other trouble that might occur that evening. He could see King Salamander some other time.

"When you described to me your sensitive disposition at dinner last night, it made me think perhaps a course of hypnotherapy would be the ideal treatment for yourself."

He had spent the interval for dinner trying not only to shut out the image of her shovelling platefuls of food down her throat but also the very detailed descriptions of what was happening inside her body as well. He had not eaten much.

"Could you tell me a bit more about what that would entail?" she asked.

"I give no medicines, no drugs. On that you may rest assured."

He noticed she looked slightly disappointed at that. A regular topic of conversation amongst the ladies was a discussion of what medicines they were taking, all seeking to outdo each other with tales of outlandish treatments and horrendous bodily complaints. Mary and Susanna often spent an evening acting out the conversations, slightly exaggerated, in front of Dominic and Isaac as a form of entertainment. Isaac had laughed along with them but at the same time carefully filed every little nugget of information away in his mind.

"I put you into a state of trance," he continued. "You are not unconscious, but you will find that you have shut your senses to everything else around you. You will be very relaxed and focussed entirely on me. I will make a few suggestions to you; for example, I may simply instruct you to believe that you are a healthy, intelligent woman. That belief will remain implanted in your brain and you will not be aware of it until you find yourself in a situation, for example sat next to Lady Rothschild, and then you will find you are able to converse freely with her."

She looked startled and slightly embarrassed at this scenario.

He knew he'd hit the mark. Susanna had attended a number of afternoon soirées and noticed Lady Carlton was always a little flustered around Lady Rothschild and would often sit there in an agony of embarrassment.

"I'm not suggesting for one moment that you experience such a social difficulty," he said swiftly; it was important to remember to flatter her. "It is just an example of how I can help you. As to any physical complaints, for example, stomach pains. My hypnosis is based on relaxation. When the body is relaxed, muscle pain is reduced and even when you come out of hypnosis, the effects remain for some time. Of course, you will need more than one treatment, but I can assure you it is worth it. Take Elizabeth Moreton for example."

"Elizabeth said you use an assistant in some way," said Lady Carlton. "Can I ask how?"

Isaac thought for a moment. He had to tread carefully. It wouldn't do to make claims that would be regarded as unbelievable, yet he had to introduce the idea of Lucy's gift.

"I am not at liberty at present to discuss Lucy's role," he said, and then allowed his voice to take on a more confiding tone. "The child, my niece, has a certain gift, when under hypnosis, to identify with the sufferings of others. I don't know whether you would call it intuition or just a heightened sensitivity to others, but she has correctly diagnosed the ailments of a number of patients."

Lady Carlton raised her eyebrows in amazement.

"Of course, you understand most people would regard such claims as trickery, fraud even, so I am currently keeping our experiments very low key. I have recorded every instance, every chance of her already having some background knowledge, everything in short that most would cause others to shout 'Fake!' This will be carried out in a strictly scientific manner."

Already, Lady Carlton's curiosity began to take over her apparent disbelief. Her eyes gleamed with interest. He could almost hear the cogs in her head whirring away as she role-played scenarios in her head, all of which would make her the toast of society.

"You say Lucy has a gift?"

"Yes."

"Would she be able to help me, do you think?" she asked.

"I have no doubt of it," said Isaac. "I could arrange a consultation here if you like; I'm sure Lucy would be agreeable."

Lady Carlton gave a slightly unhappy smile.

"Of course," he said quickly. "If you were happy with the results of your meeting, then, and again only with Lucy's agreement, we could put her talents on show at a little gathering at your house."

Lady Carlton perked up considerably. She was already creating the guest list in her head.

"Unfortunately, I am busy for the next couple of days, but I am sure I will be able to arrange something for Friday? If we say, eleven o'clock?"

"Will Lucy be available?" asked Lady Carlton.

She would be.

"Of course."

Chapter Nine

We have work to do, you and I.

Llewellyn awoke with a jolt and peered around his drawing room. The rest of the family had retired but he'd sat up for a while, thinking over recent events and slowly, in the absence of that voice, had begun to think of it as no more than a bad dream.

No. Although you'd like to think that, wouldn't you? I just thought it best to give you a little break, me time to think and plan.

Llewellyn's eyes widened with horror; to hear that voice, to understand what intentions it brought with it was surely too much to bear. Part of him still refused to believe Isaac Bercow had wrought this change in him. Could it not be a psychosis of some sort? He decided then he would not give in to it, he would fight that voice.

An interesting challenge. Are you sure you are not embarking on a path that will lead to madness, to your self-destruction?

Madness. Llewellyn shuddered. The one condition he truly feared, yet something he forced himself to face every week on his visits to the asylum. He was due to attend there tomorrow, a clinic he ran for those poor unfortunates who had left the world behind them so long ago.

You fear becoming like him, don't you?

Him? Had this trespasser in his head burrowed so deep into his mind that he discovered that shameful secret? Even Isaac knew nothing of the matter, although with his talent for discovering the mysteries of others, he would not be surprised.

No. Isaac did not tell me. I discovered him myself, that little part of him, that grain that has been lying dormant for so long, buried beneath your fears and own self-loathing. Now that is another little puzzle for you to ponder over, isn't it? Where did I really come from? Isaac, the taint, your grandfather… or yourself?

Llewellyn could stand it no more. The walls of the room seemed to be moving in on him, four walls pressing at his body, pushing it down, crushing. The sweat trickled down his brow and his hands shook. He could feel his heart pounding, his blood roaring.

He pushed back his chair, sending it crashing to the floor, and fled out into the night, not noticing how his hand, under the guidance of another, grabbed the coat and hat which would cloak him with respectability, avoid the questioning looks of others.

Catching sight of Amy as he turned to close the door, he gave an apologetic nod.

"Please, go back to bed. I have an emergency to tend to. There is no need to wait up."

Llewellyn heard his voice speak these words, saw his hand take the bag she offered, knew already he was becoming a spectator to whatever was to come that night. The maid smiled doubtfully but left him alone quickly enough. Her few hours of sleep were a precious commodity. She didn't even wonder there had been no messenger, no summons demanding his presence from a third party.

He suddenly wished more than anything that he had remained indoors, taken the sleeping draught his sister suggested when she worried at his drawn and haggard looks. Next time he would take the powder, keep the monster within imprisoned.

You are not strong enough. Now come, we have work to do you and I. A night such as this cries out for our skills to be put to their true purpose.

A solitary cab passed by. The driver, wrapped up against the cold, barely glanced at the tall shadow whose shape danced in the mists around them. The cab was empty but the driver did not seem inclined to stop.

A wise man, heading for home and hearth. What sort of mad man would be out on a night like this?

A strange laugh echoed in the muffled darkness, caused a passing market worker to pause briefly and then quicken his pace to get away from that manic sound.

Remember, let me do the talking. You just sit back, let me take care of everything.

Llewellyn could feel himself being pushed back from the world, a veil coming down, from behind which he could see blurred outlines, hear distorted voices.

You don't have to watch, you know.

But Llewellyn could not turn his horrified gaze away.

Together they walked streets that at times were deserted, at times as busy as in the daylight hours. They scanned the faces of those they passed, smiling in acknowledgement of those who recognised him with a respectful touch of the cap.

"Doctor Llewellyn!"

The voice made him pause, acknowledge the speaker. Llewellyn could sense the reluctance of his other self to stop and speak. Could this man save him?

"My dear Reverend! A strange hour for you to be abroad these streets, is it not?"

"God's work is never done," said the minister, shaking Llewellyn's hand enthusiastically, not noticing the reluctance of the other man to return his greeting. "And neither is yours, I presume?"

"*Hm?*" Llewellyn's eyes followed the man's gaze down to his bag. "Oh yes, a patient…"

"Then I mustn't detain you, my dear sir. I trust I will see you in church?"

Llewellyn had already started to turn away but stopped once more.

"I'll be there. I look forward to hearing you speak."

They took their leave and Llewellyn continued on his walk into more solitary streets.

I sense you are surprised that I choose to attend church. It should be no great wonder. Some of the greatest dissemblers, the greatest liars, are men of the cloth and that man is no exception. As soon as he gripped my hand I could feel a kindred spirit. The ministrations that he is rushing to attend to are not of the kind described in his holy book, unless you are discussing the behaviour of the fallen. The laying on of hands has a different meaning for our good minister. The performance of a hypocrite is something to be admired, to be learned from…

By now he was upon the tide of life that washed up on the shores of Spitalfields Market. Around him he saw enough depravity to make the blackness within him yearn, itch for the knife, but they were too crowded together in their filth and squalor. He needed the straggler, the lone voice in the wilderness.

"Doctor!"

A harsh woman's voice reached his ears; the doctor within recognised Amelia Palmer, a slut of a woman. The itch grew fiercer. He saw her anxious look, wondered at what she read in his face.

"Doc. 'Ave you seen our Annie?"

Annie?

"Annie Chapman. She's out tonight, earnin' money for 'er bed but she's not well… I'm worried."

"No, I haven't seen her. I'm sorry. But I'll look out for her. Do you know where…?"

"She said down Hanbury Street way but I 'aven't seen 'er."

"Please don't worry. I'm going that way, I have a patient to call on. I promise I'll look out for her."

"God bless you, Doctor. There's not many'd give the time you do to the likes of us."

Llewellyn bade her goodbye and continued on his way. The monster's itch was growing stronger, but he sensed he would soon be able to scratch it as much as he liked.

Annie Chapman. She was a perfect specimen of what he sought. He continued to walk down silent streets. Occasionally he would see a man and woman, hiding in the dark, and he would move closer before a gruff warning in no uncertain terms of what would happen if he came any closer.

Llewellyn's darkness smiled. He had no fear of such types, but this man was not what he wanted… for now. He was looking for his own little bird and soon he hoped to hear her singing. He left the couples to their fumblings and continued on his way.

Humanity flared up briefly as he passed a taproom, the doors opening to reveal the street's occupants seeking a brief respite from the grim reality of their lives. The doors closed again in response to violent curses, expelling a skirted shape which tumbled at his feet, one hand clutching a small bottle, more concerned with protecting the precious drink than her own bones.

Llewellyn leaned down and offered his hand. A nearby streetlamp gave some illumination to the woman who now peered suspiciously up at him.

"Why, Doctor Llewellyn. It does a poor girl good to see an honest soul such as yourself on a night like this."

He grinned down at her. "Hello, Annie, it's your lucky night. I've just been visiting a patient. We can walk home together."

"You'd be seen with the likes of me?" she cackled. "Wouldn't you prefer someone more… genteel-like on your arm?"

"Now then, Annie. You know me. I treat everyone the same. Let's get you home before any harm comes to you."

Her smile revealed teeth missing in her lower jaw, although the others were so black and rotten this was barely noticeable. Blood-shot flecks formed fiery rings around watery blue eyes, filthy hair hung in unruly curls around her equally filthy face. What few charms she had were long gone. Even so he gave her his arm and started towards home.

The game had begun and he was enjoying it, even as he sensed the despair of the true doctor buried within himself. He could hear the man's voice, faint accusations echoing along the neural pathways he no longer controlled. Surely Isaac would not test his power in such a way?

Oh, but he has, he will. That is the whole purpose of this experiment, is it not? You denied that anyone could force someone to commit an act against their moral code by virtue of hypnosis.

You denied that Isaac Bercow had such power, dismissed it as mere tricks and foolery, the lies of a showman, a quack. Who better to exert such power over?

If you deny this argument, then there is only one other answer. Are you sure that it is Isaac who dictates your—our—actions? How do you know it is not your true self, some inner demon who has gained temporary supremacy over your finer feelings? How do you know this is not the true you?

This argument quietened the shadow-bound Llewellyn. He did not want to face the idea that perhaps this truly was his own psychosis, that Isaac had tapped into something already there.

And when he heard those thoughts, the Llewellyn that led a trusting Annie Chapman down darkened streets threw back his head and laughed. And Annie, too, joined in the laughter, thinking perhaps by being good company he might even loan her the pennies needed for her bed.

Their laughter fed each other's good humour, causing others to smile as they passed by in the cloak of night. These sounds of life were surely a sign of better times to come on streets that had seen such horror in recent days.

Step by step, he led her back, down roads long familiar to both of them so she should feel comfortable, avoid rousing her suspicions. Step by step, on streets mostly free of the human traffic which scurried hither and thither in its daylight hours.

Step by companionable step, so that when he led her through the passageway in Hanbury Street she did not object, raised no resistance, assumed here, too, was to be found one of those patients lucky enough to have such a doctor as he, one prepared to make inconvenient calls in the early hours for little or no return. Such Christian charity was a scarcity in these times and it made her turn an even brighter smile on the doctor.

The smile stayed even as the knife scored its path across her throat, carving its way through flesh and bone with a violence that almost severed the head from the body.

And it stayed even as the blood bubbled up and out as it sought to escape the confines of artery and vein.

She lay there, at Llewellyn's feet, still with that ridiculous smile on her face as if they had shared a good joke.

Llewellyn chuckled, in that at least he could say she was right. But his hand still itched, seemed to know there was work yet to be done and he would have to move quickly. Soon the workers would be making their way towards their day jobs, feeding, filling the streets with their presence.

He stooped over the body, pulling her straight, and then he knelt over her. Quickly the knife cut through bodice and blouse, skirt and petticoat to reveal the malnourished flesh beneath. Carefully he moved the clothing aside so his work on the canvas was not hindered.

He removed his gloves and ran his fingers over her still-warm skin. Her body needed to be cleansed. And so he went to work. That was his first that night, but there would be others.

Chapter Ten

Isaac allowed Lady Carlton a little more of his time, letting her chatter idly on, occasionally making a mental note of the names she dropped with great relish, and then discreetly summoned Emily to show her the door.

He already had the bill prepared but to hand it over directly was not the done thing. He would get it delivered to her husband—to ensure payment—together with an invitation for her husband to dine with him at his club and discuss his little proposition. The lecture that evening would prepare the way for an assured acceptance.

After Lady Carlton left, he went through to his study. He had amassed a considerable amount of literature on current hypnotic theory and the views of the ancients. He was beginning to pride himself on being an expert in his field—in the area of theory anyway, and soon he hoped to be acknowledged an expert in practise.

On his desk he had a number of papers. These were his findings and future plans. He always kept his study locked. Nobody was allowed in here, even to clean, without his express permission. He would have to let Emily in soon, he thought; the dust was becoming just a bit too noticeable. He sat down at his desk and looked at his last set of notes.

It read very much like the script of play, which to a certain extent it was. His was the lead role in a drama of his own. He read through his words and sighed. It had a slightly too melodramatic tone, redolent of the music halls.

He needed to be striking, but with subtlety. There had to be a solemnity to the proceedings, a scientific authority. It had to be enough to command the respect of the men and the excitement of the women.

He pulled out his pocket watch and looked at it thoughtfully. He had toyed with the idea of changing it to a crucifix but that drew visions of cries of blasphemy, and waving a mere finger in front of a face would be boring.

No, the watch was perfect. He polished it on his jacket sleeve; he could almost see his features in the metal casing. It certainly caught the eye as it flashed in the soft glow of the lamplight that bathed his room.

He would need to ensure Lucy was kept separate from the others at the start of the event. He would have to request a small room for their preparations. It was all a matter of logistics. He gazed down at the script and started to strike out a word here, a line there, a new phrase was added, then another.

The day wore on and still he sat at his desk. When he finally stirred himself from the plans he was busy laying, it was well past three o'clock. Looking down, though, he decided it was worth it. He carefully locked his papers away and went through to the dining room. Emily had laid a cold buffet out in accordance with his earlier instructions.

As he ate, he started to visualise the evening ahead. He had the list of Fellows to hand, but he only really had to focus on one, Professor Sorenson. He thought over everything he knew about the man, which wasn't much outside his professional field.

He looked at the clock; he had hoped Eddy, one of many of his informers, would have shown up by now. He'd sent him up to Kensington to find out about the 'real' Sorenson. Every man had his secrets, and he was sure Sorenson would not prove to be the exception to the rule.

He was beginning to give up hope and trying to think of something else that would give him the bit of leverage he needed that evening when the doorbell rang. There were muffled voices and then Emily led Eddy through to him.

He was annoyed. He had given the youth strict instructions only to come to the house via the tradesman's entrance. The youth, however, was ignoring the expression on Isaac's face and was studying the remains of the meal on the table.

With a sigh, he gestured to Eddy to sit down and asked Emily to bring some more food. It didn't do to alienate his informers. He would be easy to dispose of once the time was right.

"Thanks, guv'nor," said Eddy appreciatively, as a plate of meat and potatoes was put in front of him. "I've worked up a rare appetite today, chasing around after your mad professor."

Mad? The adjective made him prick up his ears, but he was soon disappointed.

"All scientists are mad, aren't they?" continued Eddy. "Have to be to poke around bodies or inside your mind. Saw an autopsy the other week, friend at college smuggled me in. Rare turned your stomach it did." Eddy looked as though he were going to say something else but, after regarding his meal for a few more minutes, thought better of it.

"So, did you find anything?" asked Isaac impatiently.

"Oh yes, don't you fret now. It's been a hard day, but worth it. Had to spend a few pennies, mind you, to loosen some tongues."

"You were given expenses," said Isaac.

"Oh, I'm not asking for anything more—just sayin'. Anyways, found out about some fancy piece of 'is. She's set up in a place Chelsea way. Nothing spectacular to look at from what I could see, quiet sort, homely."

Isaac knew the same could not be said for Sorenson's wife. Loud and vulgar, he could never quite make out why they married. There must have been money involved along the way somewhere. This other woman sounded like the perfect antidote for marital strife.

"You spoke to her?"

"Nah, followed her home, watched her gaff for a bit, then a carriage came along and took 'er off somewhere." He shoved another forkful into his mouth.

"And?" prompted Isaac.

"I took a peek around." Isaac's enquiring look made him expand a little more. "I broke in—discreet like—round the back like you always tell me. Not a big place so didn't take me too long. Found these." He tossed a pile of letters tied in red ribbon in front of Isaac.

Picking them up, he saw they were letters addressed to a woman, Nora Feldwick. He recognised the handwriting, having had some correspondence with Sorenson.

Opening them up, he realised this was exactly what he needed. The scandal would be enough to destroy both Sorenson's career and his position in society. Eddy had done well.

Thinking quickly, he wrote a quick note.

"You will deliver this to Sorenson's when you leave here," he told the youth. "But before you go, I propose a toast."

He rose and poured out two glasses of port, passing one tumbler to Eddy. "To us," he said. "Onwards and upwards."

Eddy smiled and drank the contents of his glass down in one gulp. He never did take the time to appreciate the finer things in life.

Professor Sorenson had arrived home just after the note arrived. The missive lay innocently on the tray in the hallway. He paid it no attention at first, preferring to muse over his afternoon with Nora. They had shared a pleasant drive in the country, a meal at a quiet inn—well away from prying society eyes, and the rooms had been very comfortable. He felt content.

His butler took delivery of a package at the door and picked up the letter at the same time. Both items were brought over to the professor.

"The letter *is* marked urgent, sir," said the man.

Sorenson frowned. There was nothing in his life that could conceivably be classified as urgent at present, unless you included his desire to be rid of his wife. The piece of paper would surely not answer the wish.

He took the items from his butler and went into his study. His wife wouldn't disturb him here. It was the one rule which he managed to maintain in the house. He did his best to help his position by making sure he had as many deformed scientific specimens as possible displayed tastefully around the room. The sight of these was guaranteed to bring on one of her migraines.

He sat down by the fire and opened the letter. He froze almost immediately. It was going to be a difficult evening.

Isaac's soon-to-be-former companions likewise had a pleasant day. They were looking forward to rounding it off with a visit to the music hall. The Black Eagle would soon be open, and they had settled themselves down to a light supper at a nearby tavern before they went there.

"If only all days could be like today," mused Mary.

"You'd soon get bored," said Susanna.

"Bored? No. I reckon the life of a lady of leisure is the one for me," she said.

"Well, I've always had a hankering to take to the stage," said Susanna. "Reckon I could do as good a turn as some those that tread the boards."

"And what act could you see yourself doing?" asked Mary. "Your singing tends to frighten the birds away."

Susanna took the insult in good part. "I can see myself doing something exotic," she replied.

"Exotic?" queried Dominic. "Do you mean—?"

"No, I do not," said Susanna, offended. "I am a respectable lady after all. No, I meant something different, a magician's assistant, snake charming, knife-thrower."

"You must have a death wish," said Mary disapprovingly. "I prefer the quiet life."

"You know they do give slots to people to put on a performance, see if they can come up with something new the punters might like," said Dominic. They're doing it tonight. We could have a go if you like."

Susanna laughed with delight. "Why not? It's been a good day, and I might never get another chance."

"Now you need to come up with an act," said Mary.

"What do you mean *you*?" asked Dominic. "It's we. I think we should all do it, have a bit of a laugh. Round the day off nicely, it will."

"Then we'd better find out what particular talents we have," said Mary.

The three sat quietly for some time. This pause was deliberate for Dominic. He already knew what act he wanted to put on. For some reason he'd been unable to shake the strange notion that he would make a good knife-thrower. It was like an itch he had to scratch, a voice he had to listen to.

Strangely they seemed quite accepting of his idea. Neither fancied being locked in a magician's cabinet with swords being pushed through. Flame throwing and fire eating needed some skill, they had to admit, as did sword swallowing. Their singing voices weren't too bad, but they needed something to stand out from the crowd.

"You've got a nice, steady 'and," giggled Mary. "All the boys say so."

He glared at her.

"Take no notice of the hussy," said Susanna. "She won't be so quick to make such comments when you're aiming at her."

"Shouldn't we practise first?" asked Dominic, innocently. "There's an old warehouse down the road. Closed up for the night. We could get in easy like, nobody to see us. Then if we find we're no good we go along and just be part of the audience as we originally planned."

Mary suddenly looked doubtful. "We could get hurt though, couldn't we?"

"Not if we use stage props," said Dominic. I can pop over the theatre and pick up a few. I know a stagehand."

"I'm sure you do," said Mary, still smirking.

He gave a heavy sigh and took his leave of the women. He would be back soon with exactly what he needed. The ladies meanwhile poured themselves both another tankard of ale. The evening was going to be fun. Life was beginning to feel exciting again. They wished they had more days like this.

Isaac's carriage pulled up outside Burlington House. The roads were already busy as the cream of the nation's scientists disembarked from cabs and carriages. Peering out, he spied one or two fellows that he'd become acquainted with and then, a man he was particularly looking forward to hearing lecture, Hippolyte Bernheim. The Frenchman had been more than happy to enter into correspondence with him concerning the nature of suggestibility of the mind and its importance to hypnotism.

Stepping out into the slight drizzle that had descended on the city, he merged easily into the throng of fellows, nodding politely to those he passed, tipping his hat in the easy manner he had spent hours in front of the mirror practising. When all was said and done, everything anyone ever did was an act. The secret was making it appear natural, that you belonged.

A shadow loomed up behind him and then a hand was placed on his shoulder. Professor Sorenson was gazing down at him with a grim smile.

"Could we have a quiet word, do you think?" he asked.

Bercow looked about him. To step out of the crowd here and disappear into a dark corner would cause some disapproving looks.

"Inside, old fellow," he said with a broad smile. "Let's get out of the rain and warm ourselves through first. We could use your office, don't you think?"

Sorenson glared at him. The man was contaminating every aspect of his life.

After they handed over their capes and gloves, the two men moved across the lobby floor to the base of a grand staircase.

"Of course, I'd be more than honoured to have a look at your papers," declared Bercow suddenly in a very loud voice.

"I'm afraid I've left them in my office," said Sorenson, trying to hide his annoyance at this charade. "Would you mind accompanying me up?"

"Not at all," responded Bercow, who moved back to allow Sorenson to lead the way.

There was not the slightest look their way as they moved up and away from the gathering. The lectures were not due to begin for another hour and it was perfectly natural to see the Fellows wandering through the East Wing, their spiritual home.

Sorenson quickly found his room. He felt disinclined to offer any light to Bercow. They would talk in the dark; he did not want to see the man's face.

Isaac didn't mind. The dark held no fears for him. He might not be able to see a person but he could sense them, smell them, feel their fear or their anger—in Sorenson's case both.

"You know I have only the utmost respect for you," he said to Sorenson.

A strangled noise came from the professor's direction.

"I am about to expand my work in the field of hypnosis, bring my discoveries to the public stage, and I need your help in one small matter."

"Give your corrupt show a veneer of credibility, you mean," said Sorenson.

"Corrupt? Me? No, I assure you everything I have done has been within the bounds of scientific study. But I must admit having one of the most eminent practitioners in the field present at my first society showing would be tremendously helpful."

"You are using science for monetary gain; you are manipulating vulnerable people into believing something that isn't possible."

"Isn't possible? How do you know?" asked Isaac. "You have not seen me work, you—"

Professor Sorenson interrupted him. "There you are wrong. I had heard reports of a show that boasted both psychic ability and hypnotic control. I take care to expose scoundrels of your kind wherever I find them."

"Yet you have not exposed me," said Isaac.

"Oh, believe me, everything was planned to do just that but luck seems to be on your side. I read your letter."

Now they were getting down to business.

"I have arranged with Lady Carlton to give her a demonstration of my hypnotic prowess. I have indicated to her and her husband that you would be more than delighted to attend the event in order to celebrate the advancements in the field I am making."

Again, the sound of an animal dying in the dark.

"So I am to attend your little show?"

"Yes, but I also want you to engage Lord Carlton in conversation this evening. Stress how pleased you are that he is supporting advances in the field of hypnosis. Ensure that he completely believes what you tell him."

"Why don't you just hypnotise him?" asked Sorenson scornfully.

Bercow answered with an invisible smile. That was a good question; perhaps one day he would try it, but he couldn't risk it just yet. The easier subjects were those who were less resilient, more nervous.

"If I help you with this," said Sorenson. "Can I have your word as a… as a gentleman that you will never contact me again, or the lady in question? That you will never speak to my wife of it either?"

"Of course," said Bercow and left Sorenson alone in the room.

Both knew this was an empty promise.

The lecture hall was beginning to fill up. He was still able to get a good seat though. Near enough to catch the speaker's eye and ask a pertinent question if need be, near enough, too, for the reporter from the *London Times* to make a note of any contribution he might make.

The last stragglers entered the hall and a hush fell. A tall, broad figure moved out from the darkness of the stage and took up position at the lamp-lit lectern. Sir George Stokes, President of the Royal Society, was ready to make his address.

Bercow turned his attention away from the man; it would be a dry repeat of last year's—and the year before's—speech, with everyone laughing politely at the same jokes. His mind was occupied with the man who would be speaking after him, Hippolyte Bernheim.

The guest speaker was currently sat in the front row, flicking through some cards in his hand whilst his host talked.

Bercow studied him carefully. He looked very unassuming, but appearances could be deceptive; power could come from the unlikeliest sources.

Isaac had only just finished reading Freud's translation of his work *On Suggestion and its Applications to Therapy* and had been looking at how he could adapt Bernheim's techniques to his own. The scientist himself had been very encouraging towards Isaac when he explained how he could see the use of hypnosis in his treatment of bodily ailments, all in the pursuit of scientific knowledge, of course.

A round of polite applause brought him out of his reverie and he focussed fully on Bernheim. He noticed Professor Sorenson sat next to Lord Carlton and received a slight nod of success from him. He was now free to concentrate fully on his own role.

The Frenchman stood up and took to the stage.

Chapter Eleven

Flames could be seen coming from warehouse. Cries of 'Fire!' alerted passers-by and firemen were soon in attendance, but they did not attempt to put out the blaze. It looked too far gone for that; better to let the fire collapse in on itself and put out the flames.

Luckily, the warehouse was one of the few that stood proudly detached from other buildings with empty yard space surrounding it. There were no strong winds, so it was unlikely the fire would spread. The flames were now licking up through the darkness towards the top of the upper storey of the building. A figure could be seen at the window.

"It's old Dominic," cried one onlooker.

"What's he doing?" called another.

Everyone turned to look as the man stepped out onto a small platform below the window. He seemed to be waving and bowing at the watchers and then, with a final flourish, he jumped. The last thing Dominic heard was the roar of the crowd as they applauded his audacious feat; he was the new King Salamander. It was a pity Mary and Susanna could not stay to watch his performance.

The crowd looked stunned. To watch someone jump willingly into the flames was unheard of.

"Drunk," someone muttered.

"Or mad," said another.

A loud bang silenced the onlookers as the large supporting timbers of the building began to fall, collapsing, as the brigade men assumed it would, in on itself. No point in senselessly risking anyone's life in these cases and they wouldn't have been able to rescue the man anyway.

The following morning, Isaac was enjoying a quiet breakfast when Emily returned to the parlour carrying a note on tray. He took it and read it quickly before allowing himself to take an extra piece of bacon by way of celebration. Loose ends were slowly being tied up; he was almost there.

The clock struck ten. Elizabeth Moreton had arrived. She rubbed her hands nervously together as she sat silently in Dr Bercow's consultation room. Although her treatments were apparently doing her good, for some reason she could never quite remember what happened in this room and that thought always unnerved her. She steeled herself inwardly. *This* time she would remain aware, she would stay alert.

She had tried to convince her father she was cured and no longer needed to visit the doctor, but he had just looked at her with that irritated expression on his face he always wore whenever he spoke to her. She was his disappointment regardless of the advantageous match she had made with Sir David.

A shudder ran through her as she thought of his wrinkled skin, the veins on his hands, those bony fingers, in particular those bony fingers. What would Dr Bercow's opinion be on such a match?

She had almost broached the subject at their last meeting, only her mother's presence stopped her. Funny how she didn't mind seeing Dr Bercow in those situations, even looked forward to them, when she had such a strong sense of unease within these four walls.

Perhaps it was the decor. Would he accept some womanly advice on the matter or would he think that too forward? The rest of the house could also do with some feminine touches. She felt a slight flush rise up her cheek. She *had* to stop these thoughts.

Dr Bercow would be in soon and she needed to keep her wits about her; she didn't want these memory lapses any more, it kept her a weak and feeble woman. Dr Bercow needed a strong woman at his side.

The door swung open noiselessly behind her. She did not notice Isaac until he had reached the side of her chair. She rose hastily to her feet, blushing and suppressing the urge to curtsey. This really was too silly.

Isaac took her hand and gave a low bow.

"Lady Moreton," he said gravely.

She acknowledged him with a slight nod of her head but remained quiet; she did not trust herself to speak at present. Once seated, she had regained some of her composure.

There followed the usual questions about her current state of health, any improvements, any regressions, all of which she answered easily enough. Her mind felt alert and unclouded. *Perhaps I should ask him now?*

He had taken out his pocket watch. A heavy, silver thing, it glowed as brightly as any star. She could make out whirling lines engraved into a distinctive pattern around the edges. She tried to trace the lines, make out the shapes but it was hard. Why was she so tired all of a sudden?

The doctor was holding the watch up so it hung suspended from its chain. Just hanging and spinning in front of her. She did not speak; she had no desire to break the silence. It was much easier to allow her eyes to follow the watch, see it spin, see it swing, back and forth, back and forth.

Isaac continued to swing the watch in front of her, noting the droop of her eyelids as she fought to stay awake. She had taken care with her dress today. She was wearing the pale green silk he'd previously suggested, just a touch of lace at collar and cuffs, nothing too flamboyant.

Such touches were nice to see; they meant she was listening to him with her subconscious, that his voice, his suggestions were being followed. Better to test his theory step by step in this manner rather than go for something more theatrical and risk failure. He glanced at his watch. It was half past ten; Lady Carlton would be here shortly.

"Elizabeth," he said. "Can you hear me?"

"Yes."

"Do you understand me?"

"Yes."

A thrill ran through him as it always did when he discovered the power he held over others. She was to be the key to his success.

"I am expecting a visitor soon. You know her, Lady Carlton?"

"Yes."

"I have informed her you would be willing to give a demonstration of your talents at her next at-home. When she asks, you will say yes, won't you?"

"Yes."

No discussion, no concerns, no argument, just a straightforward 'yes.' If only everything else in his life could be so simple. Better to add a bit of reinforcement though—just in case.

"What are you going to say to Lady Carlton?" he asked.

"Yes," she repeated.

"And you will declare Lucy is an amazing creature. That you have felt her walk through your mind, examine your body from within, discover what ails you. You will do that."

"Yes," she affirmed.

Now he needed to add a little something for himself, for his own security.

"I will ask you a question when you wake, Elizabeth," he said. "You will answer yes."

Simple statements always worked best.

"Who is the man stood in front of you?"

"Dr Isaac Bercow."

"You will not be able to think of any other man but this man. You will start to think about marriage to this man."

These last instructions had become his mantra in his time with her. He had repeated it on each previous occasion, apart from the last bit about marriage. This was the first time he introduced the concept on his part. He had to make it appear natural, particularly in the company of others.

She merely said, "Yes."

"Now you will tell me about your family's business interests," he commanded.

For the remainder of their time together, Elizabeth told him, yet again, as much as she knew about the extent of the assets which her parents held and which would come to her on their death. He already knew she was heiress to a considerable fortune but he never tired of hearing it. It would not be long before he shared in that fortune.

He particularly liked the idea of having a country seat; hunting was a pastime that appealed to him. He would need a new wardrobe, a manservant, so many things to consider when a part of society.

There was a soft knock at the door. It was Emily's signal that Lady Carlton's carriage had appeared.

He turned his attention back to Elizabeth, back to the present.

"Elizabeth, when I count back from three to one, you will be perfectly alert. You will remember everything I have told you as if you had thought it yourself. Do you understand?"

"Yes."

She was gazing at him blankly, not registering he was the man over whom she should be swooning. *When they were married it would be an idea to keep her in this state,* he thought, it would make for a quiet life.

"Three… two… one."

As he put his watch in his pocket, Elizabeth seemed to shake herself as she came back to her surroundings.

"Dr Bercow, I… I… didn't drift off again, did I?" she asked anxiously.

He knew that these absences of mind were beginning to worry her, but she would never discover they were linked to his appointments. Of that he would make sure.

"No, my dear, of course not. You were merely in a heightened state of relaxation. I can guarantee you will not have a nervous attack over the next few days."

"You are sure?" she asked hopefully.

"I am positive," he said, smiling. He knew she was to attend two high-profile balls over the next few days and had been extremely anxious about being overcome in anyway. He had managed to gain invitations himself to the same events. Lady Carlton again. Perhaps a discount on his next performance for her might go some way towards showing his gratitude.

He led Elizabeth by the hand back to the parlour. Emily had already laid out a tray with tea and a plate of fancies of the kind that he knew both ladies enjoyed.

Elizabeth took her seat in a slightly dazed fashion. She hadn't completely returned to the reality of life around her. Luckily, Lady Carlton had not yet disembarked from her carriage that now stood sentinel outside his front door. He did not mind the delay; having this coach with its coat of arms proudly on display positioned in front of his house would only enhance his reputation, make sure he was taken seriously.

Lucy was already quietly settled on her stool. Even in company she remained there.

It was at that moment, however, that Eddy decided to return to the house, although thankfully he seemed to remember to go to the tradesman's entrance.

Elizabeth raised a delicate eyebrow at his appearance in the parlour.

Isaac was furious. He would have to have words with Emily. How could she allow him to come through when he had visitors. As if reading his mind, Eddy spoke.

"Sorry, guv'nor. Snuck through. Missis told me to stay in the kitchen whilst she answered the door, but I couldn't wait."

Isaac felt a slight panic. What would Lady Carlton think of finding such a person in his front parlour, and with Elizabeth present? He moved towards Eddy, ignoring Lady Moreton for the present—she still wasn't completely aware of her surroundings, and took him by the arm. He didn't try to resist. The look on Isaac's face probably suggested to him that he'd overstepped the mark.

"Alright, alright, I'm on my way. Just thought you'd like to know about Dominic?"

"Dominic?" He knew what was supposed to have happened but confirmation from Eddy would be useful… and reassuring.

"Burned last night, he did, went out blazing."

Eddy looked as though he were going to expand on his theme, but Isaac didn't allow him. That was all he needed to hear. He pushed Eddy out of the parlour and back towards the kitchen; he was practically carrying the man.

Lady Carlton's voice was getting louder. He suddenly slowed down. He didn't need to worry, did he? Lady Carlton had her own consultations with him. Anything he needed to explain away he could do so within the confines of her own appointment. She would be as easy to control as Elizabeth. He gave Eddy a final shove and sent him into the servant's quarters. Emily would calm him once she had seen in their guest.

He returned to the parlour to find Lady Carlton already ensconced opposite Elizabeth. Emily was pouring out tea and offering cakes. The women had not been left alone to talk; thank goodness Emily had some sense about her. All were ignoring Lucy.

As he entered, his maid bobbed a curtsey and took her leave, giving him the slightest of nods as she went past to indicate that all was as it should be.

Lady Carlton smiled graciously at him, extending her hand over which he gave a low bow.

"I was just saying to Lady Moreton how much I enjoyed your entertainment the other night. You brought some of my closest friends a great deal of comfort."

Closest friends. The woman was a humbug. Most tolerated her because of her marital connections; he hadn't heard of anyone who called themselves close friends of *hers*.

She was useful. A pity she was so repulsive. Her pasty complexion and puffy eyes ballooned up at him. He almost wished he had a pin so he could pop her. Time to get on with the show.

"I am glad I was able to use my talents for the benefit of others," he said.

"As should everybody who has a gift," said Lady Carlton with a pointed look at Lucy.

Lucy was smiling. She opened her mouth.

Isaac held up his hand swiftly; it was time for him to take control of the situation.

"I'm afraid I must apologise, Lucy," he said. "I've been singing your praises somewhat to Lady Carlton, in particular the empathy you have with the suffering of others. Your ability to uncover the source of their physical suffering has, you must admit, been remarkable."

Lucy had the decency to blush and lowered her eyes under his direct gaze. She really was a very good actress.

You shouldn't be surprised.

He glanced quickly at Lady Moreton. Lady Carlton caught it and was amused. Did she detect a certain *frisson* between this couple? Perhaps.

Immediately, she started to picture them as star-crossed lovers and she would be there to help them. She forgot about Sir David. In all honesty the man had not a romantic bone in his body, and he had snubbed her.

An idea caught at the edge of her mind. A little voice whispering. If the man should lose his little heiress, well, that wouldn't be her fault, would it? However, she wasn't completely naive.

"I hope you don't mind, Dr Bercow," she said. "But I've arranged for a friend of mine to come along and join us. She's suffered from a nervous disorder for some time, and the doctors have been unable to discover the source of the problem. I thought she would be a prime candidate for me to have a display of Lucy's gifts."

Isaac was annoyed. "May I remind you, Lady Carlton," he said, "this meeting was purely for discussion, for you to meet and converse with Lady Moreton and Lucy, *not* for a private showing."

Lady Carlton bristled at his sharp tone but the look he gave her kept her quiet. He was the sort of man any woman would obey, she felt. Why couldn't her husband be a bit more like him and less like the doormat he had become?

Isaac took out his watch, ostensibly to check the time against the mantel clock. He let it swing idly in his hand, back and forth, back and forth.

Both Lady Carlton and Elizabeth found their gaze drawn irresistibly towards it. There was nothing they could do to withstand its power.

"However," said Isaac. "It is also perfectly natural that you should wish to check the authenticity of any claims I might make, so should your friend appear then I will be more than happy to facilitate such an examination. May I enquire as to the person's name?"

"Miss Darpole," said Lady Carlton.

"Ah, I do not believe I have had the pleasure," said Isaac. He smiled at her. "Perhaps the very reason you have chosen her?"

She blushed guiltily at his comment.

Isaac was relieved. Dominic's research into Lady Carlton's life had included a breakdown of all her friends, relatives, creditors, and servants. Miss Darpole was someone on that list and, even better, someone he had looked at in detail. She had aroused his interest as a possible alternative to Lady Moreton, should Elizabeth prove resistant to his charms. Her considerable dowry was a very attractive proposition.

"My dear Elizabeth, you yourself have said you would like the opportunity to help the more unfortunate members of society. As well as the poor and the destitute, surely we should also include those in our own strand of gentility who are suffering in some way?"

She nodded. "Of course," she said. "I hate to think of anyone suffering in pain and misery day after day." She looked at Lady Carlton. "And no one has yet made a diagnosis of what ails the unfortunate woman?"

Isaac rose. "Excuse me ladies," he said. "I just need to instruct my manservant to prepare for this evening's excursion."

He left the room swiftly before Lady Carlton could begin to cross-examine him. He would have worked up a cover story by the time he got back. First, he made a quick diversion to his study, scanning the card which held Miss Darpole's details. He couldn't afford to make a mistake. It was the work of a moment and he was soon heading back to the parlour, spotting Emily heading in the same direction. She'd probably heard the carriage and was coming to inform him.

"Emily, I've just been informed we are to expect Miss Darpole. Please could you organise another cup and a slice of that almond cake?"

Obediently, she retreated to the kitchen whilst Isaac rejoined his clients.

Mere minutes passed before Miss Darpole herself was admitted, Emily providing the extra refreshments at the same time. Though she was of an age with Elizabeth, that was all they had in common. He could not really describe her beyond being a blob, a silk-clothed blob, but a blob, nonetheless.

It would take a brave fortune hunter to engage themselves to this creature.

"My dear Miss Darpole," he exclaimed, fixing an admiring glance to his face. "I am honoured you should join us today, although I am sure you would wish that it was under different circumstances."

She beamed at him, her huge cow eyes blinking as she tried to focus. Vanity prevented her from the using the pince-nez that dangled at her neck.

"You know Lady Moreton, I presume?" he said.

Miss Darpole smiled benevolently on Elizabeth. Even without having used his tricks on her, Isaac could read her mind, saw the dismissive way she looked at Elizabeth, the intrigued look she cast his way. She was falling under his spell and he hadn't even done anything.

Isaac looked at the three women and he knew, just knew his enterprise would succeed. Lady Carlton had been looking for some way to make a splash in society, and he would be the means by which she achieved it. The other two? Well, they were indulging in foolish fantasies that, whilst flattering, would not succeed in any way with him. He had taken out his pocket watch again. Lucy saw the watch and focussed on him completely.

"Lady Carlton, Miss Darpole. I am now going to carry out the demonstration you desire, but I must ask that you do nothing without my permission. You must not interfere in any way. Do I make myself clear?"

His fierce tone and steady gaze drew subdued responses from them.

"I will firstly put Lucy into a mild hypnotic state. This is necessary to remove external distractions from her senses."

He started to swing the pocket watch, back and forth, back and forth. Lucy's eyes followed it but he knew she was shamming. From the corner of his eye, he could see his small audience also following the movement of the chain. Back and forth, back and forth.

Would they also go under, he wondered? They were obviously highly suggestible women. It would be quite an achievement but the future engagement he desired depended on an independent and clearly remembered exhibition of his powers.

Go on, urged his voices.

No. Isaac was still determined to do as much as he could on his own terms, in his own way. It was a matter of pride.

"*Of course*," said Genesis, understanding, reasonable, unexpected.

He needed them to see everything clearly, for there to be no confusion. Theirs were the words that were to be carried out into society.

He made a small movement with his hand. A cufflink glimmered. Its sparkle distracted the gaze of the women. This small action achieved its aim and broke the spell that had started to weave its way into their minds. An alert, and suspicious, look appeared on their faces. That would do. Better to win over a cynic than an already converted fool.

He turned his attention back to Lucy.

"Lucy, my dear," he said. "I need you to concentrate now."

"Yes," she said.

"Who is in front of you?" he asked.

"Miss Darpole," replied Lucy.

"Have you ever met her before?" he asked.

"No."

Isaac looked at Miss Darpole and she inclined her head in agreement with Lucy's words.

"Now, Lucy, look into Miss Darpole's eyes. They are your windows to her soul, the door through which you will enter. Do you understand?"

"Yes." Her gaze had become intent to the extent that Miss Darpole looked uncomfortable under this visual examination. Isaac noticed.

"Miss Darpole, I must ask you to remain absolutely still. Do *not* look away from Lucy."

Lady Carlton looked on, enthralled, wondering at what could be going on in their minds.

"Lucy, I need you to look further into Miss Darpole's mind. What do you see?"

"I see darkness," said Lucy. "The blood runs freely but there is a point where it stops, where it enters a darkness I cannot probe."

Her words sounded suitably intriguing; they were well-chosen. He had spent some time crafting the responses she would make, and they had spent even longer rehearsing them, not always with the right amount of decorum, he recalled.

"You need to look deeper, Lucy," he commanded. "Let your spirit move freely within her. Travel her nerve endings, push onwards against any resistance. Go!"

Miss Darpole almost shot back from Lucy at this but a look from Isaac kept her in her place. Lady Carlton's mouth was open in a small 'O.'

"Tell me what you see now, Lucy."

She shook her head. "It's hard, so hard to push through this darkness; I don't think I can do it."

"You must try, Lucy. You need to keep going."

He let Lucy continue to bore into Miss Darpole a little longer. Then, just as it looked as if Miss Darpole could no longer continue to bear this examination, Lucy closed her eyes.

"Lucy? Why have you closed your eyes?"

"I do not need this earthly sight to discover what troubles Miss Darpole," said Lucy simply. "My mind is able to reach into hers unaided. I have come to the source of her problem."

There was an audible gasp from Lady Carlton. Miss Darpole looked slightly shocked but remained still.

"What do you see now?" he asked, somewhat more gently this time.

"There is a growth. I can see that it is in the stomach wall. It causes pain when the stomach tries to digest anything."

This time Miss Darpole did move; she shot a look at Lady Carlton giving a slight nod of her head as she did so. She was about to speak but Isaac held up his hand to stop her.

"Remember, Miss Darpole, I cannot allow you to speak. To do so would open me up to accusations of trickery. I would be accused of giving you leading questions, gleaning information from your answers. You understand, both of you?" He included Lady Carlton in this directive.

They both nodded their acquiescence once more. He turned his attention back to Lucy.

"Now, Lucy, we need to be more precise; what else can you tell us?"

Lucy concentrated hard and then spoke again, her voice soft, almost childlike.

"The growth is a cyst. It is not harmful on its own, but the harm comes from its position. It is growing and is starting to block the lower intestine. Muscles cannot contract fully and they are thrown into spasm; this is causing Miss Darpole's discomfort."

"Lucy, you have done well. I ask you now to withdraw from Miss Darpole, slowly, though, gently."

He gave her a minute to compose herself, her breathing steady and regular, in and out, in and out.

"When I count back from three you will be alert to once more to those in the room and everything around you. You will remember what you have discovered about Miss Darpole's condition. You will be calm and free from anxiety. Now, three… two… one."

Lucy opened her eyes and blinked.

She certainly is an amazing actress, thought Isaac with approval. She had struck just the right note of innocence and knowledge. He also noticed Lady Moreton's attention focussed upon himself, an adoring gaze that was not lost upon Miss Darpole who immediately sought to break the spell.

"Quite the lady's man." The voices laughed.

"Dr Bercow," Miss Darpole said tremulously. "I feel rather light-headed. I beg your pardon, but some water?"

"Of course, Miss Darpole," he said, solicitously pouring a glass and holding it for her as she took a sip.

Lady Carlton looked slightly impatient. She wanted to get to the crux of the matter. She wanted to know if Dr Bercow and Lucy were the genuine article, if Lucy were too good to be true.

"Well?" she demanded. "The diagnosis?"

"From what Lucy says, I would propose that Miss Darpole seek out an independent doctor's professional opinion and ask that he pay particular attention to her lower abdomen where he will find evidence of the growth of a cyst. It is not malignant. However, should it be allowed to continue to grow then it will obviously have serious consequences for her future health."

Lady Carlton smile, a self-satisfied expression on her face. He knew he had been successful.

"My dear?" she asked Miss Darpole. "Is Dr Bercow correct?"

The lady in question nodded.

Isaac raised his eyebrows. "So you know what is wrong with you?" he asked in feigned surprise.

"I apologise for the subterfuge," interrupted Lady Carlton. "But I needed to be sure. You can appreciate that, of course?"

"Of course. I take no offense. After all, you have a reputation to uphold and there are plenty of disreputable types attempting to batter down the doors of polite society." He smiled obsequiously at her. Isaac hated to crawl and curry favour, but he was still dependent on patronage for the time being.

"I had an examination yesterday," said Miss Darpole. "His findings were just as you described. Lucy truly has a formidable talent, or at least a strong sense of empathy for the afflicted."

Lucy remained quietly in her place. She had performed her role and Isaac was pleased. It was time to let her mind wander.

Chapter Twelve

Once the women had left, Isaac sat in quiet contemplation. His time was coming; he could feel it. The sneers and condescension of others that continued to sound in his ears whenever he mixed with his peers would be silenced for good. Each step he took on his journey towards the destruction of the Threlfal family was a step that filled him with joy. There was nothing he wouldn't do, nothing he couldn't do.

And he was achieving a large part of it on his own, regardless of those creatures Genesis had lodged in his head, regardless of Lucy.

Regardless, regardless? It would be interesting to see how you fare should we fall silent. How do you know what is truly earned from your own efforts? Take care Isaac, you may be fooling yourself.

But Isaac ignored the warning, preferred to smother it beneath his vanity.

In daylight he could not see them, just hear their murmur, and he had learned to shut them out as he concentrated on whatever task was in hand. They were quiet for the present, as they always were when he had been successful, yet he could still feel them nearby. Sometimes it unnerved him.

It had taken him a long time to get used to them, to accept they were to travel with him. But there were times when he would listen to them; it eased the pressure, allowed him to function normally. At other times, it showed he was in control, regardless of what Genesis hinted.

He took a key from his pocket and moved over to the Chinese cabinet, pausing only briefly before inserting the key in the lock and turning it. The bottle stood there, black and plain, hiding its contents from the curious eye.

He took the bottle and released the stopper, savouring the aroma of his holy water. The green spirit, once poured, shone like a liquid emerald. He held it up to the light, enjoying the purity of its appearance. A jug of water stood, but he would not dilute the drink's power.

He locked the parlour door and drew the curtains. Emily would not disturb him. Seated by the fire, he stoked the flames to ward off the early afternoon chill.

Now it was time. The first sip burned, its fire flaming its way down to his stomach. He took another sip, this time enjoying the warmth that bubbled away inside him. The room grew dim around him.

He tossed back the remains of the glass and placed it on the side table. Now he would let his monsters, his brothers, talk to him. He called them brothers although he had never seen them. They spoke in so many languages, yet he could understand every word.

Initially he could only hear a babble, a steady murmur that rose and fell, then finally one voice came out clearer than the others. He gazed into the fire and allowed himself to listen.

That was the other thing he had learned. To listen to them in the small hours. If he tried to shut them out completely, they would push and push at the edges of his sanity, creating an unbearable pressure. Times like these eased the tension. He understood it was also their way of exerting their control over him, reminding him that he *did* need them, despite his pride.

If anyone else came into that room and found him they would have assumed he had fallen into a doze. The room was silent apart from the tick of the clock and the crackle of the fire. It was as if the parlour had separated itself from the rest of the world.

The voice was stern, commanding. He had to focus. Through the swirl in his mind, he allowed his instructions to settle, ignored the fact that it was Genesis speaking, controlling him despite his own illusions.

A smile spread over his face. He only had to wait until Sunday night when he took Lucy to perform at Lady Carlton's home and he would be able to move forward. He had to ensure he recorded his findings properly, though; the Society would not accept his theories without that. He was a serious scientist despite the mauling his last paper had received.

A trickle of sweat ran down his cheek; the fire inside him flared up as it always did at this point. This always preceded his dreams. This was where he found his monsters. They roared and moved around inside his skull. He could feel them beating behind his eyelids, pushing, thrusting, trying to force their way out. Unlike the day, the night allowed him occasional glimpses of them. He wondered if he had ever met any of them in real life.

"*Perhaps*," said Genesis. "*Like often flocks to like.*"

But for some reason, Isaac felt tonight was going to be bad. He could feel the pressure building up within him, his head almost ready to explode. He opened his eyes and felt in his pocket. The opium would help. It would soothe him and he would be able to sleep, sleep his monsters away until the next time.

He roused himself and took the powder with the water he ignored earlier. Opening the curtains, he noticed dusk was beginning to fall. Passing Emily on his way up to bed, he instructed her not to disturb him for the rest of the evening. In fact, it would be better if she took the night off, even go and pay her mother that visit she had been unable to make earlier.

"I would have to stay overnight, sir," she said doubtfully.

"That's no problem," he said. "You've worked hard lately; you deserve a break."

She bobbed a curtsey and returned downstairs. He knew it would be a little while before she left; she was a conscientious soul and would be making sure that everything was right before she left. And she never asked questions.

She doesn't need to.

That brought him up with a start. Had Genesis spoken to her? Lucy? No. He could not worry about her now. Another time.

He lay on his bed, closing his eyes to the evening gloom. Images of Dominic burning floated through his head, of the knives cutting into Susanna and Mary as they struggled against Dominic's hold, of the sense of shock, horror, and surprise that arose in them as they fought in vain to free themselves.

He did not feel remorse over their deaths; they had been necessary. Still the images came though, fire and flesh, skin and smoke, all provided courtesy of Genesis, he had no doubt. He could almost smell the acrid stench curling up through his nostrils.

His hands involuntarily beat at his bedclothes, smothering the invisible flames until finally the vision receded and he was able to sink into the darker world of sleep. Here, too, there were visions, equally disturbing if he had been conscious of them, but they were talking directly to his inner self. He dreamed on.

When he eventually awoke, darkness had well and truly fallen. The monsters, however, had not gone away. One in particular was howling at him, scrabbling at his eyelids with its sharp claws. He would have to go out. This was the monster he would have to allow to walk tonight.

In the absence of a more permanent host for his voices, he had discovered that giving himself over to one of them would also bring relief. He disliked being used in this way, but it kept them quiet. It even made him feel a stirring of sympathy for Llewellyn.

"Good choice," murmured Genesis.

Isaac got up and splashed some cold water on his face. He noticed his eyes were red-rimmed and slightly puffy. That was no matter. He would not be going anywhere where such features would be remarked upon, indeed they would be seen as normal.

Wrapping a scarf around his face, he set out into the night, leaving the house by the back door. Looking behind him, he saw all was darkness. Emily had gone and she would have instructed the cook to leave as well. Whatever happened later, it would not make its way back to these walls and taint what he had worked so hard to achieve.

He was in a small alley, hidden from the view of his neighbours. Their houses were lit up by the soft glow of lamplight; figures moved to and fro inside. Sometimes he envied them their easy lives but then the thought of the sheer dullness of everyday life pushed him on down the path he had chosen in preference. He could tolerate many things, but boredom was not one of them.

Something howled inside his head. He looked up and saw the moon glowing down on him in all its virginal beauty. There was a magnetism there; he could feel its pull and so he started to walk.

Keeping to alleyways and byways he moved inexorably on, down towards the river, back towards the East End. He thought he had left the place behind but obviously it had decided it was not ready to let him go. He allowed the moon to pull him onwards, guiding his feet he knew not which way.

He did not yet know what he was going to do, how this particular monster was going to walk. All he knew was it was pushing harder, pressing on his thoughts, growling its distress, its need for release. Nerve impulses sparked in rapid succession, caused him to pause and blink unsteadily. Small white flakes started to sting at his eyelids. Snow. Not a blizzard but enough to warn of worse to come.

He had only passed one or two souls so far on his solitary walk but soon he would be back in Whitechapel amongst the nightwalkers and nightcrawlers. His gloved hands were tingling. They were ready. He could feel the monster inside, it was starting to emerge, stepping out newborn in this depraved world. Tonight, this monster would walk.

"'Ello, guv'nor," came a sing-song voice nearby.

He turned and looked. A young woman was stood near the lamppost, a tattered shawl covering a worn gown. He frowned and she saw.

"Well, you ain't to everyone's taste either," she snapped at him, understanding the unspoken rebuff.

He continued to stare at her. Scarred cheek and missing tooth, he wondered how she thought she could continue to ply her trade with those looks. Then again, drink played tricks on the mind as much as she turned tricks in the street. She was a mess that needed cleaning up.

"'Ere, what you looking at? If you ain't interested be off with you, otherwise I'll charge you just for looking!"

He laughed at the conceit of her. She really thought she was worth looking at?

"I'm truly sorry, my dear," he said. "It's just that you really are a sight for sore eyes."

His voice must've reassured her, well-spoken; indicating he must have a bob or two.

She batted her eyelids in what she thought was a flirtatious manner but which merely made her look as though she had something stuck in her eye. She moved closer to him, looking up under the brim of his hat, into his eyes. He smiled down at her and she stood there transfixed.

"I know a place we can go," she said softly. "Come on, my boy."

She took his hand and led him down the side of a building towards a low archway. He allowed himself to be moved further into this maze, noticing its familiar twists and turns.

"Here," she said and opened a door. "It's been empty a few days. Noticed it a little while ago. Reckon the tenants have done a flit."

He looked down the hallway to the door beyond.

"Can't get in there though. Blinkin' big padlock on that door."

"What does the landlord say?" he asked curiously. This would be interesting; he'd paid the landlord until the end of the month, so he had no need to visit his tenants before then.

"Who says I spoke to the landlord?" she said, grinning up at him.

"Quite a resourceful woman, aren't you?" he said, lowering his scarf. He pulled her unresisting towards him. Stroked the scar on her cheek, allowed his hand to trace its way down her neck. Moved it to feel the nape of her neck.

He could smell the reek of her, see the dirt in the folds of her skin. His monster was walking now. It was almost with amused detachment that he pondered on how the creature inhabiting him would deal with this one.

He watched his hand as it tightened itself around her neck, feeling the curve of the bones under the skin. She had gone pale beneath the dirt. Her eyes had widened and terror started to etch itself into her features. Her mouth opened but no sound came out because at that moment Isaac rammed his fist into her mouth, shattering teeth and jawbone.

He could feel the growl rising up in his throat, the sight of blood calling to the monster that now walked. He drew back his lips in a snarl and then leaned in to her neck, ripping and tearing at the flesh, letting one monster devour another.

Eventually the growling subsided. The monster, sated, left Isaac and he drew back from the mangled body that lay at his feet. He withdrew a small flask from his pocket and swilled its contents round his mouth before spitting it out onto the floor. The headache had gone and his mind was quieted.

He took a deep breath and then bent and picked the woman up. Looking out onto the narrow street, he saw the snow was falling thickly, keeping everyone indoors with their windows shuttered and covered. A disused wharf was not far away; he had been able to consign earlier victims to the tender care of the tides of the Thames without ever meeting anyone. Tonight turned out to be no exception, the fortuitous snowfall camouflaging his movement.

Once back at his old lodgings, he set to, lighting a fire to boil up water to scrub the floor. Where she had stood had, thankfully, been on a piece of old carpet, easily torn up and burnt. Some marks remained, some stains, but that was the way of many of the buildings in this neighbourhood. When seen, nobody asked questions.

He would stay here tonight and return to his town house in the morning. Despite the fire, the rooms felt cold and damp. The silence here was stronger than he had experienced earlier. Perhaps because where there had previously been four there was now only one.

He used some of the water to wash himself down and then he threw his coat onto the fire. Beneath his old bed was the coat and bag he had carefully packed away before he left. He pulled out this coat and shrugged it on. It was identical in every way to the one he had just burnt. Placing the bag on the bed, he went through its contents.

Here, too, was a small black bottle. He felt the strong urge to take another drink but knew that to do so might call forth another monster and who knew what form that demon might take.

He did not have the energy for a second such event on a night like this. Luck would only hold for so long. Instead, he lay down on his bed fully clothed and pulled the blankets over him. As he drifted off into sleep he thought he had better remember to give the landlord another month's rent on the morrow. There was still some use to be had from these lodgings.

The savagery of what he had done did not disturb him in anyway.

How can it? said Genesis. *You were merely being yourself.* And he laughed into the void, his triumphant howls failing to disturb Isaac.

He rose early to complete whiteness. Looking out of his window, crusted in rime both inside and out, he could see nothing but white as far as the eye could see.

He quickly dressed and tidied his rooms before leaving them safely locked up behind him. Walking down the hallway, he glanced briefly down at the floor, knowing that something had happened there, but he wasn't quite sure what. There were stains which hadn't been there before and the carpet had been ripped up.

His keen senses smelt death. It was not enough to change his mind about retaining the rooms, however, and he went out into the cold morning with a lighter step.

"Dr Bercow!"

The cry came from behind him. Isaac turned and saw Old Jack, standing in his doorway, pipe in hand. The man had never showed any real curiosity about Isaac; again, it paid in these parts to know as little as possible about your neighbours, but he had taken in the odd parcel for him or made an occasional delivery.

"Jack," he responded with a cheerful smile.

"Just wanted to say how sorry I was to hear about your companions. Dreadful business, dreadful."

Isaac set his expression into one of regret. "Thank you. Yes, it was, truly terrible. I couldn't face coming back here the other night. Last night though… Well, you learn to live with these things."

Jack nodded his agreement. "Ar, tragedy strikes in strange ways. Glad to see you're still around, though. Comforting to know we've got a respectable doctor in these 'ere parts."

Isaac inclined his head in thanks at this compliment and took his leave. He wondered briefly if there was any sarcasm in the man's last comment but then thought better of it. Old Jack knew the ways of the street, he had to, to have survived this long. He was not the sort to make subtle comments that might be hazardous to his health.

Isaac had in fact treated him and a few others around there for various ailments, free gratis. Part of his charm offensive to keep them friendly, and it seemed to have paid off.

He had to try a different approach in Waverly Road. Having money and position went hand in hand with a genuine suspicion of anybody new aspiring to their ranks. Having carriages with crested badges waiting outside his house was a first step in this. Once the twitching curtains saw that the great and the good were beating their way to his door, then the invitations would start coming.

The roads had not yet been cleared and so far no carriages had attempted to make their way down them, so he was able to make his way in relative safety back to the main thoroughfares. Young boys with shovels and old men with brooms were sweeping their way along the pavements.

To be the first to walk on such mornings meant he did not have to walk in the muck of others. The cold clear air was bracing; his mind felt alert and refreshed. He tilted his hat back and lowered his scarf a bit so his face was no longer obscured. He did not need to hide from anybody.

On the main roads, carriages were slowly beginning to make their way along. Trade and commerce had to continue even on days such as this. An empty hackney cab went by, but he did not hail it. Isaac was enjoying the walk, the strong pulse of his blood as it circulated through his body. Exercise was necessary for a healthy constitution.

The door opened as he mounted the steps to his house in Waverly Road. Emily stood there smiling, ready to greet him. He had not expected to see her back so early.

"I've just arrived," she said with a smile. "I thought if I set off early, I would be back in time to light the fires before you rose."

He smiled back at her. "That was very kind of you, but I really expected you to stay a bit longer with your mother."

She gave a sigh. "To tell the truth, after the first hour, she did nothing but moan. I was glad to get away. You are up early today, sir, aren't you?"

"Woke early, couldn't get back to sleep. And you know what it's like when you see the snow, don't you? You want to be the first one to make footprints."

She laughed. "I know that feeling, sir. Anyway, I've got the fires going and I'll get your breakfast on now if you'd like."

He nodded his thanks and went into his study. Unlocking the desk drawer, he pulled his journal out. He noted down yesterday's date and started to write. When it came to recounting the events of the evening his mind went blank. A sudden realisation hit him. *This must be what it is like for my patients. A chunk of their life gone with no recall available, only a vague sense of something.*

"No time to be developing a conscience now," whispered Genesis.

When Isaac had finished, he started a fresh page, on this he drafted out his plan for the day. He would do this each day, he decided, and then when he came to write it up he could check against what he had done, see where the gaps occurred, keep track of himself.

He put this into practise and for three days found that he had done everything he had planned to do, been everywhere he had planned to go; there were no gaps. He breathed a sigh of relief.

It was now the Friday before the exhibition he was to put on at Lady Carlton's. Lucy would appear soon. It was time to rehearse their routine. Elizabeth Moreton was also due to arrive. When

Emily opened the door, however, it was not to admit just Elizabeth but also Lord Moreton, Lady Elizabeth's father.

"Sir Michael!" he exclaimed. "What a delightful surprise."

"Dr Bercow," replied Sir Michael coolly. "My wife is unable to chaperone Elizabeth so I thought I would come along. Find out exactly what you *do* during your consultations. I take it you have no objection to that?"

"None, none at all," said Isaac smoothly whilst mentally calling his patron every name under the sun. "You have already seen the results of my treatment; the hysteria from your daughter has been suffering is rapidly disappearing. Our remaining consultations are merely to reinforce this."

"I also wanted to discover how *exactly* this girl… Lucy… is to aid you in your exhibition at Lady Carlton's tomorrow. I spoke to Professor Sorenson at the lecture the other night. He was surprisingly complimentary."

Isaac wondered at what Sorenson's precise words might have been, but he doubted it would be anything damaging. There was, after all, the matter of keeping a certain scandal under wraps. Sir Michael's next words reassured him.

"I believe in the advancement of Science," said Sir Michael. "If my family can help in anyway then I will do all I can to promote your cause. I just need to make sure that my daughter has not been duped. Lady Carlton has also relayed the events of Miss Darpole's examination by yourself back to me. I must say I have been pleasantly impressed."

The old bag hadn't been able to keep her mouth shut after all, mused Isaac. Word would be buzzing round drawing rooms and parlours today as visiting cards were issued and returned. There would be a highly curious audience tomorrow night.

He settled his two visitors into their chairs and then pulled his own chair in front of Elizabeth's. He made sure that he kept a modest distance from the girl. So far she had barely acknowledged him; he had often noticed how in the presence of her father she became subdued and silent. Perhaps he could do something to redress the balance in that respect before their consultations ended.

"Firstly," he said, turning to Sir Michael, "I put your daughter into a trance. She is still conscious, but she is in a relaxed state with only one point of focus… me. Once she has reached that stage then I start to give her instructions which she retains in her subconscious memory. These are simple commands, like *'Look strangers in the eye,' 'If you feel panic breathe deeply,'* simple little commands that help her control her anxiety."

"And this girl?" Sir Michael nodded at Lucy, submissive as ever on her stool. "What is her role in all this?"

"If we encounter any problems… call them a blockage if you like… Lucy is able to interpret your daughter's thoughts. Talk her through them so that our consultation can continue. A sympathetic female presence is often reassuring to my patients."

"I was told that she… enters… the minds of others. Is that possible?"

"I leave that for your own eyes to judge, Sir Michael," said Isaac, dissembling. "I make no wild claims, only ask that my results speak for themselves. Any little theatrical touches are for entertainment purposes, you understand."

Sir Michael nodded, satisfied at this eminently sensible answer, he would be aware that Isaac had to put on a show to entertain as well as to cure but all in the most respectable manner.

He was a tall man who towered over Isaac when he was standing; in fact, he towered over everybody he met. This domineering persona was something that Isaac felt was at the root of Elizabeth's hysteria. He was not unhandsome, though, and Isaac noted that at a dance, the ladies often tried to catch his eye despite his married status. There was something of the bear about him. Isaac had so far been unable to uncover any infidelities on the part of the man; the skeletons that Sir Michael hid were resolutely staying silent.

He took out his watch.

"A fine specimen," said Sir Michael approvingly.

"My father gave it to me," said Isaac. "A family heirloom. Now I think we should begin."

He started to swing the chain. Back and forth, back and forth. Elizabeth followed it as she always did, her eyes moving obediently from side to side, following the silver as it flashed across her field of vision. Back and forth.

"Your mind is relaxing, Elizabeth," said Isaac gently. "Allow yourself to let go. Your eyelids feel heavy. Close them. Your muscles are tense, relax them. Your hands are clasped, unwind them."

He continued to swing the chain in front of her even as her eyes closed. Her eyes moved from side to side beneath the lids, following the invisible currents of air that the swinging watch displaced.

"Still yourself, Elizabeth," he ordered, his voice slightly firmer this time. "Fix your eyes on a point deep within yourself. Take your mind into that safe place within you."

Her closed eyes no longer moved.

"Now I am going to give you a series of commands. You will repeat each one after me. Do you understand?"

She nodded.

"You will obey these commands whenever you are nervous. Do you understand?"

Again she nodded.

"Elizabeth, when you enter a room full of people you will walk in with your head held high. Tell me what you will do when you enter a crowded room?"

"I will walk my head held high." She even straightened her back and tilted her face upwards as she repeated these words.

"And when you meet a stranger, you will not be scared, you will not be flustered or upset. You will smile and look at them openly with perfect ease. Elizabeth, how will you react when you meet a stranger?"

"I will smile and look at them openly. I will *not* be scared." Her jaw set slightly; her whole posture gave her the appearance of a woman totally in control of herself. Except she wasn't.

And so it went on, all harmless, all deserving of nothing but Lord Moreton's approval. Isaac went through their mantra as they had done many times before. This had been created in response to the complaints that Sir Michael had made against his poor daughter.

Her father meanwhile sat there nodding his approval. Isaac could tell he was fighting hard against the impulse to follow the watch as it swung back and forth. His eyelids were drooping and starting to close, soon they were shut completely.

Isaac had finished Elizabeth's commands. He had noticed Sir Michael's demeanour from the corner of his eye. Could he find a skeleton now? Was it worth the risk? Another thought crossed his mind and he smiled.

"Put him under," murmured the voices. *"Let us take a look."*

An hour later he roused both Elizabeth and Sir Michael from their trance. Sir Michael looked slightly confused and embarrassed. Isaac waved this off.

"Don't worry. You looked a little fatigued when you arrived. I thought I would let you doze and refresh yourself. I think a light refreshment for us all wouldn't go amiss."

He rang for Emily who swiftly delivered the little pastries that he had discovered Sir Michael had a weakness for. The man was now looking at him with a more favourable expression on his face. It was obvious he was thinking something over. Isaac waited.

"Dr Bercow," said Sir Michael eventually. "I wonder if you would care to join us for dinner this evening?"

Father and daughter were both smiling benevolently at him. They didn't seem surprised that this invitation had been issued.

"It would be a good opportunity for us to get to know each other in a more sociable setting, don't you agree?"

"That is very kind of you, Sir Michael. I would be honoured to attend."

The consultation had gone completely to plan. Isaac was looking forward to the evening.

Chapter Thirteen

The door was opened to him by a powdered footman. His hat and coat were taken with the utmost politeness and he was led to the drawing room where he was announced with the appropriate ceremony.

As well as the family, Sir David Threlfal was also present. An annoyed look crossed Sir David's brow as he acknowledged Isaac's arrival. The quick look that passed between him and Sir Michael did not go unnoticed by Isaac. There was something of an atmosphere in the room and he was sure it had to do with himself. He wondered how his influence could have worn off so quickly.

He walked across the room and bowed low over Lady Threlfal's hand. She accepted his salutation somewhat nervously and avoided his eyes.

Stories of my hypnotic powers are probably swirling by now, he thought with some amusement. They probably considered one look from him and they would be enslaved forever. Oh, if only he had such power. He wondered at the relationship he and his future mother-in-law would have.

By now, Elizabeth had moved to his side and was smiling up at him. There was no fear there, only an open and frank countenance that one wouldn't have seen even a month ago. The blushing, tongue-tied social disaster had all but disappeared.

"Dr Bercow," she said, "I am so glad you could come this evening."

"I am honoured to have been given such an invitation," he replied smoothly, looking across at Sir Michael as he did so. A loud *harumph* came from Sir David's corner. The man was doing everything he could to avoid Isaac short of complete social rudeness.

"We were talking," said Sir Michael, "of the power of the mind over the body. I was mentioning your techniques and how they have been used for the good of my daughter. All this achieved by suggestion and implementation of self-belief without recourse to drugs."

"Hypnotism depends on the susceptibility of the client," said Sir David. "I regard it as dangerous that the most vulnerable members of society would be putting themselves at the mercy of a predatory practitioner."

Isaac bridled at that. "Are you saying that I am predatory?"

"No, no," said Sir David. "I am saying that there are *some* predatory types out there always looking to seek advantage. I am *not* saying that I regard you as one of those." His eyes, however, belied his words.

"But don't you think that unlocking the mind can be a powerful tool in a person's ability to repair themselves?"

"I do indeed, Dr Bercow, and that is why I am so concerned there should be strict guidelines as to how such therapy is practised, including its use as a public form of entertainment."

"You are referring to tomorrow's engagement at Lady Carlton's, I assume?" Isaac enquired.

Sir David merely gave a slight nod. His eyes fixed unblinkingly on him. The doctor refused to be intimidated by this and returned his stare.

"I would not call it a public entertainment. It is merely a few friends of Lady Carlton's acquaintance who would like a consultation away from the stigma of attending a doctor's waiting room. Everything that happens there will be treated with the utmost confidentiality."

Sir David frowned at him.

"I have agreed to attend this consultation freely. I thought it useful to show our friends what *can* be achieved," said Elizabeth as the two men continued to glare at each other. "My father has also given his consent."

Sir Michael smiled at Sir David. "I am sure there will be no problems," he said. "Dr Bercow has done nothing but good for my Elizabeth, you can see that, can't you?"

Sir David gave his grudging assent but refused to join in any further conversation despite the ladies' attempts to introduce topics that could not possibly cause any disagreements between those assembled.

The party that was eventually summoned to dinner entered that room in a somewhat subdued state. The ingestion of good food and wine did, however, go some way towards relaxing the tensions between the men so that once the table was cleared and they separated from the ladies, even Sir David had been restored to almost good humour.

The three men sat quietly smoking their cigars for some time before Sir David finally spoke up.

"I am not completely against hypnosis *per se*," he said, looking at Isaac once more. "To be able to improve or cure mental instability or a physical ailment without recourse to drugs or painful surgery is a laudable achievement."

Isaac took a sip of his brandy, allowing its warmth to spin its way through him. He had finally begun to feel relaxed. Sir David's comments showed no sign of his earlier dispute.

"Provided of course it is carried out by a reputable practitioner."

Immediately, Isaac was back on his guard.

"David," warned Michael.

The man refused to catch his friend's eye.

"I was wondering where you trained," he said. "I mean no medical college that I am aware of has taught you, I have seen no certificated evidence of your qualifications."

"David."

Again, the warning. Isaac had the feeling that this was the conversation that had been conducted in the drawing room and which he had interrupted on his arrival. He was prepared for this, however, he always had been.

"I have my certificates from the University of St. Andrews which I will happily furnish you with if you would care to call on me at my practise in Waverly Road."

"Strange," said Sir David. "An old friend of mine, Dr Havers, is currently visiting and he has taught at St. Andrews for a number of years. I mentioned your name to him and he cannot recall anyone of your name attending whilst he was there."

"I was there," replied Isaac calmly. "Dr Havers was not, however, one of my assigned lecturers or tutors. I would be more than happy to meet him at your convenience so that we could clear up this little matter that vexes you so."

Sir David looked somewhat surprised at this. He had obviously expected fluster and indignation, not the calm assuredness of Isaac's response.

"We thought Lady Carlton's gathering would be a suitable venue for your re-acquaintance," he said.

Now that did worry him, but he could not afford to give any outward show of this. With his usual practised calmness, he merely smiled and nodded his agreement. He would think later. A solution was bound to offer itself when he meditated on the problem at home. For now it was better to not let it show it bothered him.

The rest of the evening passed quietly enough. He was flattered by the attentions of both Elizabeth and her father who assured him in most emphatic tones he was to feel free to call on them *any* time. Sir David's eyebrows shot up at this but he refrained from making any comment. The battlefield had been declared, and the time of engagement; Sir David would leave anything else to the events of tomorrow.

When he finally returned home, Isaac was starting to consider this problem of tomorrow.

He needed his brothers, his monsters. He regarded them as his now, completely forgetting Genesis had delivered them to him. They were there, whispering quietly in the background. They would not come forward and speak, however, unless they wanted to. At these times he had to go to them.

He unlocked his cabinet and poured himself a glass of absinthe. In the past he limited himself to one drink of this spirit a week; however, recent times demanded that he speak to the brothers on more frequent occasions. Theirs were the voices he needed to hear. He refused to admit he was losing control of events.

When he had drained the contents, he heard them speak.

"*The easiest solution is to ensure that neither man makes it to the engagement*," said one.

He had heard this voice earlier, a hinted suggestion as soon as Sir David had indicated his intentions. It was this hint that brought on an element of panic. How was he to see it through?

"*You could let another monster walk*," said another voice.

"*Free their chains*," said another.

"*Free their chains*," grew the chant.

His mind was dark; there were shadows there. One day he would be free of these companions of his, but until that time came, he could use them.

He took a paper of white powder and mixed a solution which he hastily swallowed. Then he allowed himself to relax in a chair and waited.

A knock at the door disturbed him. He'd forgotten to tell Emily she would not be needed. He stayed silent and shut his eyes. If she opened the door and saw him, she would not disturb him any further.

He heard the slight creak of the door, a light footstep and gentle breath over him. Then, a voice, a man's voice. It was with some effort that he restrained himself from opening his eyes.

"Is this the man?" he heard Emily's voice, timid and unsure.

"Yes, that's my doctor." The voice belonged to Dominic. But how was that possible? He was supposed to have died in the inferno at the warehouse. Perhaps the papers had got it wrong. And if it was him, did he know? Did he realise the part Isaac had played in orchestrating his death?

"Shall I wake him?"

"No, leave him be, I'll return tomorrow."

Their footsteps retreated and he heard the door close once more. He would have to tread carefully, but the powder was beginning to take effect. He could feel this particular monster scratching to get out; sharp dagger points stabbed at his eyes, sliced at his skin. There was burning, fire, raging heat. What would this monster be capable of?

Let us find out, murmured Genesis. *This one is special.*

Chapter Fourteen

"Sir David," Isaac groaned. "Sir David."

The monster had to walk but there was a price to be paid for its freedom; it had a task to perform.

"*Better the monster than yourself,*" said Genesis. "*Let him go; he knows what to do.*"

"*Let him go,*" said another.

"*Let him go, let him go, let him go,*" they all chanted, their voices rising to a crescendo as the monster continued to birth itself, to push and push against the barriers of Isaac's mind until Isaac couldn't hold him in any longer and with a final gasp, the monster opened his eyes.

The room around him was unfamiliar. This monster had been kept in the dark for a long time. *It is a nice room,* it thought. Warm, comfortable. But he didn't belong here. He belonged in the gutter, amongst the thieves and the murderers. That was where he had to return to, but first he had to go somewhere. There was a name he remembered. Two names. Dr Havers. Sir David. First, which one would he visit first?

The one who can destroy our name, said a voice. The monster cocked his ear. He heard these voices sometimes, their murmurings penetrating the darkness in which he had been buried for so long. He knew they had influence over his keeper. He knew he had to protect his keeper.

"*Dr Havers,*" whispered the voice. "*Dr Havers.*"

Dr Havers. He would have to sniff him out. Find the scent of him somehow. He went out into the night, forgetting to put on an overcoat but not feeling the cold. A passing night watchman gave him a curious glance but walked on quickly without making a comment.

A glow of light suddenly shone out over him. Turning, he realised it was the servant. She was looking worried and holding out his coat. He didn't need it.

"*Take it,*" said the voice. "*Don't draw attention to yourself.*"

"Sir," called Emily. "Sir."

With a feigned smile the monster returned up the steps and allowed her to help him on with his coat.

"Don't wait up… Emily," he said.

She nodded her obedience, but he saw the doubt in her eyes. He waited until she had gone back inside, then he turned up his collar and headed out into a cold winter night yet again. As he walked, he would pause every now and then and sniff the air. There was a scent there, somewhere, drawing him on, pulling him further towards the townhouses of Kensington.

Dr Bercow had engaged a room there at his club. It was one frequented by some of the most eminent members of the Society.

The voices were telling him Dr Havers would be staying there. He kept on walking, his eyes bright and staring ahead, the smell getting stronger. Occasionally, a beggar would look as if they were about to approach him but one look at his eyes and they would drop back swiftly.

A Hackney cab stopped at the roadside. He paused for a moment, in two minds as to whether to take the carriage. As he approached, the horse started and shied away. The cab driver struggled to gain control over the animal whilst apologising to Isaac at the same time.

"Sorry, guv'nor," said the driver, cursing loudly at his horse as he pulled at the reins. "Don't know what's got into the nag, would you…" His voice trailed off as he looked into the monster's eyes. What he saw there the monster didn't know, but it was sufficient to shut the man up, for him to mumble excuses about a fare he had forgotten and move swiftly off, the horse settling the further away they travelled.

The monster looked after them for a moment then once more sniffed the air; he turned and continued his way on foot. When he finally reached the club, most of the members had left or turned in for the night. The doorman looked slightly surprised to see him at that hour but respectfully bowed and guided him in.

The monster looked in the dining room first. Even in the early hours there would be some service here, strays wandering in from a poker game somewhere or a ball; all such miscreants required feeding. Was Dr Havers such a miscreant? He could smell him strongly now although the man could not be seen.

He returned to the lounge and saw a white-haired, corpulent-looking figure sitting near the fire, nursing a generous brandy. He had seen him before, that was why he could still remember his scent. This monster fed on smell.

Dr Havers had spoken to Dr Bercow once at St Andrews, he remembered his keeper had been delivering a body to him. Did Dr Havers know anything more about his keeper than that? The body had nearly been rejected, there had been suspicion about where it had come from, but Havers had been in desperate need and in the end this had overridden his misgivings.

"Dr Havers," said the monster.

"I… I'm sorry?" said Havers, looking up at him. "I don't believe I've had the pl—" He stopped, apparently uncertain as to whether to go on.

The monster could see him beginning to remember, an unhappy, but uncertain expression appearing on his face.

"Allow me to reintroduce myself," said the monster smoothly, listening to the voices in his head. They told him what to say; that would make it easier for him. He needed that help; words were not his area of expertise. Thinking was difficult.

"I'm Dr Bercow. You are due to attend an engagement of mine tomorrow, I believe?"

Dr Havers looked at him, light slowly beginning to dawn as the name pulled out the memory of his correspondence with Sir David Threlfal. There was something about being a fraud, but…

He looked again at Bercow. The man was vaguely familiar, yet this was the man he was supposed to denounce. It would be best to let him speak, keep it pleasant before any accusations were made. Besides… the glint in the man's eyes looked dangerous, though he was safe enough in the club.

"I believe so," said Dr Havers. "Please, sit down. Let us remake our acquaintance here in private. Much better than the sort of public showdown I believe Sir David is after."

He wasn't quite sure why he had said that. Yes, he was. This man was dangerous and Havers was a coward. Better that Threlfal took the blame.

He rang a bell to the side of him and a waiter appeared, carrying the brandy decanter. Another glass was swiftly produced and filled.

"I propose a toast, Dr Bercow," said Dr Havers, raising his glass. "To science and the search for truth."

The monster raised his glass in acknowledgement and took a small sip. It slithered down his throat, the taste familiar and welcome.

He allowed himself the moment to enjoy his drink, ignoring Dr Havers' examination of him, fully aware of the intensity of his gaze from behind his glasses.

"I do believe we *have* met before," he said at last. "Although I still cannot quite remember teaching you."

"You are quite right," said the monster easily. "You did not teach me. I was in old Brighting's classes, although I did manage to attend one or two of your anatomical lectures, but these were so well attended you probably overlooked my face."

Lies, so plausible, were practically dripping from his lips and Havers was lapping them up.

"Probably, probably," said Dr Havers. "The lecture hall was always packed when I performed a dissection. Quite often there wasn't even any standing room left. It is not beyond the realms of impossibility that I did not notice you.

The monster raised his glass to the firelight, swilling the purple liquid round so that it sparkled warmly. A deliberate action which drew Havers' attention so that he was watching the current, the whirl and tide of the brandy dancing in its glass. Then Bercow lowered the glass, allowing the spell to be broken.

The monster was satisfied. He had got the signs he was looking for. The man was tired, susceptible, even a little afraid.

He took out his pocket watch. He had watched this procedure from behind Bercow's eyes many times now and always wondered at the ease with which others succumbed to its pull. Now he had to perform the manoeuvre himself.

He let the watch dangle absently for a moment, allowing its silver heaviness to distract Havers. He would have to be careful. Dr Havers would be aware of David Threlfal's complaints of charlatanry, of his use of hypnosis.

He took the fob into his hand and flipped open the case, making a pretence of checking the time and adjusting the hands. Then he allowed it to swing in his hand once more, a distracted expression kept carefully fixed on his face. He studiously ignored Dr Havers for a while, taking another sip of his brandy, before absently looking up at his companion again.

"Oh, forgive me, Dr Havers," said the monster. "Please pardon my rudeness, but it has been such a long day and to sit here in the warmth, with a brandy and pleasant company, that is something to enjoy."

Dr Havers smiled easily at him. He had noticed the watch, waited for the man to start swinging the object in front of him but he hadn't done. He had merely adjusted it and now it was hanging idly from his hand. Spinning slowly on the chain, round and round and round…

The man was right, a warm fire, a good drink, pleasant company, what more could you want on a night such as this? There was one thing, but he couldn't mention her name here. Sir David was mistaken.

"Sir David was mistaken," said the monster.

The words came easily. "Sir David was mistaken," asserted Havers, smiling genially at him.

The monster was no longer holding his watch; that had been tucked away unnoticed. Instead, he held a small crucifix on a delicate chain. The chairs on which they sat had high wing-backs, completely hiding them from the view of anyone else that might be in the room. They had kept their voices low so likewise their conversation could not be heard. The monster hung the chain up in front of Dr Havers.

"Beautiful, is it not?" he said as it swayed in his grasp. "So delicate; like human life, it hangs here, in the balance."

"It looks as though it could be easily broken," observed Havers, unable to tear his gaze away.

"Which is why I take care of it," said the monster. "It has great sentimental value to me. The young Lady Moreton gave it to me earlier today, as a token."

"You have an understanding with the young woman?" asked Havers. He felt no astonishment at the man's declaration. It felt… *right*.

"With her *and* her father," said the monster, continuing to swing the chain.

Havers was entirely focussed on the delicate filigree work of the chain, trying to follow its intricate weaving as it moved. He had to concentrate, as the monster knew he would, to see how the pattern spiralled down the metalwork. Back and forth his eyes moved, back and forth the chain swung. Another brandy was poured and placed in his hand. He took the drink as he was bid, relaxed back into his chair, closed his eyes…

When the monster finally left him, Havers had been put in complete remembrance of his earlier meetings with Bercow. It had been as the young man had said, in crowded lecture halls on a couple of occasions. He could even recall his colleague Dr Brighting mentioning his name in rather glowing terms. Bercow had definitely attended St. Andrews. He had been mistaken and would correct this accordingly at Lady Carlton's. Such a pleasant chap, Bercow.

The monster got up and departed. He did not intend to spend the night in the club. The voices had guided him and told him he had done well, now he had permission to hunt. He left the club, this time remembering to don his overcoat, and stepped out into the early morning darkness. He had a couple of hours before dawn. Enough time to allow the blackness of the night to conceal whatever action he should take.

He sniffed the air, inhaling the smells that assaulted him from all directions until one forced its way to his attention above the others and he started to walk.

The aroma took him back towards the East End and down to the river. He passed sailors and matelots, some working, some fighting, some drunk; he ignored them and walked on.

He could feel the saliva start to fill his mouth as he walked; an enterprising pie vendor had opened his shop early—or kept it open late—to attract late night customers such as himself who would be hungry after their evening's exertions. This man was looking hopefully at the monster as he passed—custom had probably not been that good and he was about to close up, but one last sale might turn the evening into a success.

The monster approached him, certain his well-off appearance would reassure the pieman, encourage him to think he would make more than one sale. He stifled a laugh as he pictured himself handing food to the hungry and the homeless down by the docks. No, that would never happen.

He ignored the wares on sale at the window and pushed past the shopkeeper. He would choose his own pie from inside, he told him. He didn't want something that had been going stale in the night air for the past few hours.

The monster took care to shut the door behind them. The smell of meat and gravy was strong in his nostrils but he craved something else, something more. It was like an itch that he had to scratch or it would not go away. An old cleaver lay on the countertop, obviously well-used. He wondered how sharp it still was; he needed to find out. He lifted it up, ignoring the pieman's request to put it back. It felt heavy in his hand, satisfyingly so.

A movement behind him alerted him to the pieman, who had started to step back towards the door. He smiled reassuringly and picked up one of the pies from the counter. It was still hot and gravy was starting to seep through the poor pastry but he ignored the burning of his hand.

He walked towards the pieman, holding out the food as if in offering. The other man relaxed somewhat, he had made a sale, there was nothing to worry about, nothing…

Boiling gravy and congealed meat forced its way down the pieman's throat. He tried to swallow, to spit it out, but was unable to empty his mouth, and as he coughed and spluttered, he reached out to the monster.

The monster saw the hand come towards him. *Something to test the cleaver on,* he thought and he raised it. Down it came, a satisfying splice; the cleaver was good. It needed more exercise.

He swung it again and again. Eventually, when he felt his blood begin to cool, he stopped. The man's body lay in various parts around him. That would never do in a pie shop.

He walked over to the counter and pulled out the large roll of greaseproof paper kept there for wrapping pies and meat. Carefully he packaged each piece of the pieman up and placed it on the counter, then he turned and walked out of the shop, again ensuring that the door was closed behind him and the 'shop shut' sign prominently displayed.

Chapter Fifteen

Glancing down at himself, the monster noticed the stains on his coat; luckily it was dark and so not too obvious. He broke the ice on a horse's trough and purged his face with the freezing water. The cold made his face glow and his heart race.

"Mad," muttered someone as they passed him by, but he ignored their comments. The opinions of others didn't matter to him. He knew there was something else to do, somebody he had to look for.

Another voice was speaking to him, travelling across time. Genesis. His master. He knew he had to listen to that one voice above all others.

"Don't worry, my son," said Genesis, soothing, reassuring. "I know the presence of others confuses you, that you are a solitary creature, but soon you will gain your freedom. Look for the doctor inside yourself; he will direct you."

Genesis could so easily have instructed the monster, guided his steps, named his target, but that would have been to excuse Isaac. The doctor, now hiding silently in the darkness, shielding his eyes against what was done in his name, had to be complicit in these actions. Only then would he acknowledge the part of him that Genesis held.

This was the hidden evil, the part Bercow declared resided in all men, the part that demanded relief, release to prevent even greater horror. He had never considered the extent of the evil that originated in a man in the first place. In some men, they already held the greatest of monsters.

"Do you recognise yourself, my dear doctor?" asked Genesis. But he knew Isaac wouldn't answer that yet, could not contemplate the true nature of himself.

Meanwhile the monster continued to search for the doctor. It was hard trying to think when your mind was cluttered with the voices of others, their opinions, their desires. He tried to find his keeper. Dr Bercow was in there somewhere. He turned his gaze inwards, searching the dark shadows, dismissing the drooling mouths and burning eyes of the other monsters; his actions that night had fed them well, given them an appetite for even more. Then he heard him, his voice calling to him, softly, gently.

"Dominic," whispered Isaac. "Dominic."

The man who had burned, thought the monster, *yet escaped from the flames*.

"Find him," said Isaac. "Find out what he intends to do."

"Kill him?" asked the monster, feeling the heat rise within him once more.

"No," said Isaac. "Not yet."

He hoped that decision wouldn't come back to haunt him, but he needed to know how Dominic had survived, what he knew. Did it mean Mary and Susanna would also turn up? There was no way they could know what he had done to them; it simply wasn't possible.

Unless, unless… no, he was a good hypnotist. No, there was no way they had pretended to go along with his hypnosis. It worked, it really worked. He knew it did.

Or was everyone pretending? Was he being mocked? He felt a sudden craving for the reassurance of his hearth, of drink, of the poppy. He began to change his mind about Dominic; the man would have to die… again but not tonight.

Two deaths in one night would be suspicious. The monster could not cope with that. He had to instruct him carefully. There was hardly any time left before the sun struggled its way back against the night sky. But already he was running out of time, his influence waning. He could take over, push forward, reclaim his body… but coward that he was, he wasn't ready to face the world yet; instead he would remain hidden for a while longer.

The monster had made its way back to the old lodgings. A lantern shone in the upper window, but when he went in, there was nobody there. The doctor's bed and few belongings had not been touched.

He moved through to Dominic's quarters where the lamp shone in the window. There was no sign anyone had been there. The bed was still made and the room was empty of any of its occupant's belongings; these had been disposed of by Bercow before he returned to Waverly Road that morning.

The same went for the women's rooms. For the first time, the monster felt unnerved. He could not see anything but he could sense someone's presence. He sniffed. Smell was often more reliable than sight. He smelt burnt flesh, no, *burning* flesh.

He moved back through to the kitchen following the aroma. Still there was nothing. A flash of light in the window caught his eye. He moved over and peered through the grubby panes. The smell was stronger now.

With a tug the monster grabbed the warped frame and pulled it up. The cold night air swirled in and around him. Ignoring this assault, he put his head out and glanced across the roof tops.

He could see something that looked like a spark, jumping from roof top to roof top. The smell of burning flesh was coming from that direction. The spark paused and then carried on dancing, this time coming back towards the monster.

It was getting closer, the acrid stench getting stronger, but still the monster kept watching. He was not scared of this demon, whatever it might be. Nearer now, leaping gracefully from guttering to ledge to windowsill, the burning vision came dancing towards him. And Isaac refused to look. To do so would be to recognise Hell.

The monster barely recognised the face of the man, blistered and shiny; he had obviously burned and burned for a long time. His features had started to melt and merge into one another. He had become a molten candle of a man. This dance though? Who had taught him this dance?

By now the flame had reached his own window, its heat pushing him back into the room. The monster and the demon. Who had created them?

"You look at me and wonder," said the man once Dominic.

"I have seen you before," said the monster.

Dominic shrugged. "Many have seen me, usually mine is the last face they see."

The monster was uncertain. This was no man. He was something else, an entity.

"Listen carefully," said Genesis gleefully.

"This is the time when the monsters walk," said Dominic, looking on the monster with an almost friendly air. "We create madness and mayhem wherever we go, remind our keepers what a fragile hold they have on life."

"Our keepers," said the monster. "You have a keeper."

"I did have," said Dominic. "He was claimed by the fire though."

"So you no longer have a keeper?" asked the monster, puzzling this over.

"Yes. I have been freed forever," said Dominic. "Would you like to remain free? Not have to go back into your shadows. Not have to listen to those voices. Not have to worry about a fleshly body."

The monster thought. Yes, he would like that. He did not like the clutter in his mind, he felt pressured and controlled.

"I can help you," said Dominic. "It will take time though. I know that he is listening. I can see him looking out of your eyes. There is fear there."

The monster knew he was right. He could feel the doctor pushing his way back through the fog of his thoughts, demanding to be heard, demanding to reclaim his rightful place in the real world. If the monster went back this time, if Dr Bercow was back in control, would he ever let him walk freely again?

"He won't come back yet," said Dominic. "Not here after the trouble earlier. He won't want to face what he was responsible for. You still have time before he comes out."

The monster was confused. He needed the voices. They would tell him what to do.

Genesis? Master?

He could feel Isaac's thoughts pushing forward. The anxiety of the man as he battled to regain control.

"I am your keeper," he heard the doctor say. "Without me you will not survive."

"You will look after me?" asked the monster. "You promised me my freedom."

"And you will have it again," promised Isaac. "I just need you to stay with me for a little while longer."

Could he trust the man's words? The doctor had let him out and he had done his bidding.

"Trust me," whispered the man.

"Trust him," whispered the voices, mocking the doctor.

The monster knew he would have to obey. If he did not, he did not know what the creatures inside his head would do. When he gained his freedom, he needed these voices to be quiet, stilled.

The flame was wavering in front of him. The fire spirit that was Dominic seemed to be fading. It was as if the breeze of the voices in the monster's head was blowing Dominic out of existence. He was disappearing, spluttering.

"I will come back for you," he promised. "I will relight the fires of myself and burn the hell of our lives away."

The monster looked into the coal eyes. He could see nothing but darkness. A black pit of nothing at the centre of this burning frenzy. Then he was gone completely.

Just as the flame disappeared, so did the monster. His self-doubt had given Bercow his way back into the real world, regaining control of his body. Ever the man of science, nonetheless he felt completely shaken. What he had seen could not be real.

Genesis had a hand in this. Was he deliberately trying to drive him mad? Bercow was doing his bidding; why would he try and sabotage his plans? No, this must have been hallucination brought on by his earlier indulgence, there could be no other explanation.

But then he glanced down at the cuff of his shirt. Blackened and frayed, he lifted it to his nose and sniffed. The smell of burning still hovered.

He walked quickly to the window and looked out. There was nothing there. He slammed it shut and returned to his bed, sitting there with his head in his hands as the parish clock chimed the hour. He was still there when the sky had lightened, as still as a statue with no evidence of life.

When the clock struck noon, he eventually roused himself. He needed to recover quickly. Pull himself together. Tonight, he had an engagement on which so much of his future success depended.

He had to throw off these doubts, these hallucinations, focus his mind. He stood for a moment in front of his wash mirror. He would need to clean himself up considerably before he ventured outside. His eyes were bloodshot and his face covered in an early morning shadow.

Shave, wash, change. It took some time before he looked once more like the respectable gentleman that he always aspired to be. He was able to step out, however, with some degree of confidence, nodding amiably to his former, and now once more, neighbours. Like before, they did not ask too many questions. Better to know nothing.

Today, he broke with his usual habit and took a hansom cab back to Waverly Road. He did not want to exhibit himself abroad when he needed to focus. Arriving at his townhouse, he was initially unable to get a response to his ringing of the bell.

Irritably, he cast his eye up and down the street. Just as he was considering going round the back of the house, Emily came running up to answer the door. She looked flustered.

"Oh, sir," she cried. "I was so worried when I found your bed unslept in last night. I went out making enquiries. I've only just returned."

"Where?" he asked sharply.

"The apothecary," she said. "You go there early to get your powders some time. I thought that would be a good place to start… I was discreet, sir."

"Anyone else?"

If she had gone to the Moretons', or God forbid, the Carltons', it could do untold damage to his reputation although he had a memory of going to his club. If that was the case, he would be remembered, it would prove a useful alibi.

Alibi? Why had he used such a term? It implied a crime. He felt confused again. Such moments were becoming too frequent. The monsters. He had thought if he freed them, if he allowed them to roam, it would relieve the pressure he felt.

The one he had released last night was caged once more inside him. His presence was heavy though. He was moving around inside his head. A dull roar of words he could not quite make out. There was anger there and fear. How could the monster fear him?

He moved past Emily without further comment and locked himself in his study. He needed to keep the world out.

"Speak to me," he whispered silently. "*Tell me.*"

There was a murmuring. They were coming to him. They were real, yes, they were real, he wasn't mad, he couldn't be…

And yet it was a child's voice that spoke up first. And Isaac cried out in fear and terror. This was no monster gifted by Genesis, this was his own blemish, his own taint. Something he had buried so deep he had almost forgotten. It had been many years since he had heard that voice. A childhood nightmare.

The first time he had killed.

Isaac had not given him a thought from that moment on, even though prior to the boy's death they had played together nearly every day when they could get away from their chores. An accident, everyone had said, and he had not disabused them.

Watching the life go out of someone had not disturbed him, especially when that person spoke to him, reassured him death had not been the end. The boy had remained his constant companion, a voice in his head since that time but as it had merged with the others, he had forgotten his name, who he had been. He had become almost nothing but now he demanded to be heard.

"Isaac," called the boy in his high-pitched voice. "It is you who has created these monsters. They need to be released once and for all. If you keep them, they will destroy us. They will destroy you."

The fear he had earlier felt at being taken over completely by the demons housed within him rose up in violence. Not only were they causing chaos in his world, they were also destroying any sense of reality within himself.

"How?"

"They have already started. They are already looking for me, I… I don't have long."

"What will they do when they find you?" asked Isaac, shaken at the apparent warfare that was occurring within his own mind.

"They will turn me, make me one of them. I will become a monster."

Isaac shuddered. What would the boy monster demand of him? What revenge would he exact for the life he had taken? And why had Genesis sent him this boy's soul with the others—or was it his own conscience at last speaking up? Isaac no longer knew.

Everything was changing. His plans had gone awry. Dominic had returned; the monsters were flexing their muscles. He needed to clear his head. There was one person whom he trusted to do that.

He had not seen him for some months, but he was the only one he could think of who would give him the relief he desired.

He glanced at the clock. He did not have time to make the visit he craved, that would have to wait until after the engagement. He would have to wait but he already felt calmer; he had made a decision, he had a plan. Everything would be alright. As he relaxed, the voices in his head faded and the pressure upon his brain eased.

Feeling lighter in body, he started to prepare himself for the evening ahead. He rang down to Emily. She would draw him a bath. Tonight, he would be clean in body as well as in mind. He had to give Sir Michael and Sir David no excuse whatsoever to adjudge him anything other than a gentleman, an honest citizen, a reputable scientist.

As the afternoon wore on, he found his equilibrium restored and with it his confidence. *I have to be outstanding tonight.*

He would show Dr Havers what he was truly capable of, astound him so completely that those memories of himself as a grave-robber would remain buried forever. How completely had anyone ever taken over the heart and soul of another? He knew he had taken ownership of Elizabeth, but he had to show how fully she obeyed him whilst demonstrating his skills in the field of hypnotherapy.

An idea slowly began to form in his mind. By the time the clock struck five, telling him it was time to dress, he knew what he had to do. There was a very slight risk involved, he felt, but it was insufficient to stop him.

"You are ready?" he asked Lucy. He had started to avoid her lately, hating the mocking look of her eyes, the knowledge she held within, her link to Genesis. One day perhaps…

The girl stood behind him. Demure in silk and pearls, her hair shining in the flicker of the lamps. She was almost beautiful but not quite. If you looked into her eyes, you could still see the ugliness there.

"Of course. Tonight you will achieve amazing things," she said. "Genesis is very pleased with you. You have fed his monsters well."

She gave him her widest smile and he trembled.

A carriage had been hired to take him to the Carlton residence; an extravagance but necessary to indicate he was a part of this society. Once he had married, he would have the means to summon a carriage whenever he needed. That was a day he looked forward to.

"Genesis will give you a gift tonight. He knows how you desire to demonstrate your power, that you wish to show you can separate mind and body, that one can be released from the other on mere instruction. He will allow you to do this."

Isaac felt a thrill at this, even as part of him feared it was another trick, another step on his road to madness. Last night's events were pushed firmly to the back of his mind. Tonight would be his night. All that suffering, those unfortunate deaths, the lapses of memory, perhaps that had been Genesis's trial to see if he were truly worthy of the power he desired, of being a true servant.

Lucy opened her mouth, but it was Genesis who laughed.

The door opened for him with a flourish. The butler led them through to the drawing room and they were announced in clear, ringing tones. Everybody stopped and looked at them. He didn't mind. He allowed them to look. Let them see who Dr Isaac Bercow was.

Sir Michael and Elizabeth had already risen from their seats and were coming over to greet him. They were both smiling and Sir Michael had extended his hand. Dr Havers was seated next to Sir David, but Isaac saw no sign of animosity there. He was amongst friends, almost, he decided as he studied Sir David's complexion.

The man still didn't look friendly but neither did he look as if he were going to make a scene.

After a brief exchange, Lady Carlton came up to him and took possession of him as was her right as the hostess for the evening. He prepared himself for a round of banal pleasantries.

It was during these seemingly nondescript conversations that he often found information, read between the lines of the lives that he would shortly be exposing to others. As he absorbed all this, he smiled and nodded behind his veiled eyelids.

At dinner, he sat between Elizabeth and Sir Michael, an arrangement that drew knowing looks from the ladies further down the table. Lucy was entertaining Sir David and apparently enjoying every minute of it, unlike Sir David.

It was a pleasant meal, but he felt strangely separate. He knew he had to convince the watchers of his abilities. Genesis had granted him his wish; tonight he would finally try something he had never attempted before, but if it worked, well, he would be the toast of society and if it didn't... no harm done.

But first he must prepare.

"You understand, ladies and gentlemen," he said. "My young assistant needs to be able to relax. She must be in an absolute state of calm before we proceed."

This element of separation added to the drama of the occasion; he could already feel the sense of expectation flowing behind them as they left the room.

He did not want Lucy to speak to anyone else in the company; part of him feared she was already probing minds, setting other plans in motion for Genesis, plans of which he would be unaware and might affect his show.

"And you think removing my physical body will achieve this," she chuckled.

He doubted it but it made him feel better to have this moment of separateness when he could visualise the events ahead, regain his composure.

He had observed the gathering; a small file lay on his desk at home containing their names and the ailments that various family members and friends suffered from. He had been able to commit them to memory with no real difficulty—a photographic memory could be a blessing as well as a curse.

Isaac knew that Lady Carlton had an ailing godson. This boy was to be the centrepiece of his exhibition.

"We have good company tonight, Lucy, truly deserving of something amazing." He rubbed his hands in anticipation, again thought of Genesis's promise.

"Tonight, I have planned a treat for them. I will show them the true power of the mesmerist, *my* power, in all its glory. After tonight I will be fêted in the greatest houses in the land. My fortune will be made." He allowed a self-satisfied smile to play on the corner of his mouth.

"I need absolute obedience tonight, Lucy. I have made discreet enquiries about our patient. The boy is Sir Meecham's only son and heir. A weakly fellow, nobody has ever been able to say quite what's wrong with him. Even the best doctors of Harley Street have drawn a blank but tonight *I* will cure him."

It was not a boast he had made out loud before, even though there was only Lucy to hear him, but he felt the rightness of it. He knew that he *would* cure him. The certainty he felt was complete. He had been told it would be so.

But he needed Lucy's obedience. How would she respond to hypnotism, he wondered.

"You could try." Genesis. Challenging him.

He took out a small silver crucifix and started swinging it idly in his hands. Lucy's eyes opened as he did so and started to follow it, back and forth, back and forth. He kept the motion going, noting how the pupils of her eyes had dimmed as she focussed, how all expression seemed to have vanished from her. She was almost ready. He had only one question, one command for her.

"Lucy, who must you always obey?

"You."

And then she laughed. As did the voices in his head. As did Genesis. And he knew he had failed. That he had no control over her or any of them. But they were bound together, an invisible wire that tugged remorselessly at him. He could never be separated from her or Genesis either in life—or in death.

"Time for us to go now, Lucy," he said, resigned, taking her by the hand and raising her up. Better to see this through. See what would happen, what Genesis had in store for him.

Lucy was once more biddable and unresisting and allowed him to lead her to the door.

They walked arm-in-arm back to the drawing room, making their way through the semi-circle of chairs that had been gathered and down to the front, then he turned and faced his audience.

He took his time as he gazed upon their faces; some looked at him with frank curiosity, some with contempt, some with interest. Occasionally, he would meet a glance and return that person's stare until they looked away. He would not brook any challenge to his supremacy tonight.

"My lords, ladies, and gentlemen," Isaac began, hands raised, a conductor guiding his orchestra, a role he relished. "Prepare yourselves for a true marvel. Never before has such a feat been seen in our great city or anywhere else in the world. Only here will you witness true psychic ability. Watch and wonder."

There was a slight raising of the eyebrows from Sir David at that. His little speech did sound somewhat flowery but tonight he couldn't resist goading the man just a little.

He pulled out the chain and started to swing it innocently back and forth in his hand. From the corner of his eye, Isaac could see Lucy retain her concentration on the object. He needed to make sure that there was no eye contact between her and the audience, he had to fade them out.

"I understand that we have a young patient tonight. Lady Carlton, will you bring the young man forth? He will need to be seated between Lady Moreton and my assistant, Lucy."

Lady Carlton rose with an air of self-importance and left the room. Silence fell as she returned with the boy. He was led forward, a gawky lad, pale and graceless, a poor specimen indeed.

She seated him in the chair Isaac had indicated.

"Tonight, for the first time ever, you will see the soul of one person enter the body of another." He paused dramatically. "Tonight, the soul of Lady Moreton will depart her body at my command and enter that of our patient. Under Lucy's guidance they will examine his vital organs, his blood, his emotions. Then they will return from their journey and we will finally know what truly ails this child."

He saw with satisfaction the boy's startled look, his disbelief easily read. There were stirrings amongst the company. There was a murmur around the room. Isaac raised his hand for silence. It came in an instant.

"Yes, it is hard to believe," said Isaac, the puppet master, surveying his audience with a look that settled them immediately; he had almost got them, too, under his spell. "But I will demonstrate both the truth of my claim *and* cure the boy in front of your very eyes. Watch and prepare to be amazed."

He gave a low bow and turned away from them… towards Elizabeth. She was smiling trustingly up at him, complete and utter faith written on her face. He had never brought her any harm before.

Her father, too, had approved the part she was to play in that evening's demonstration. Isaac had explained that some elements were just showmanship for the titillation of a society that was easily bored. They both understood fully that it was Lucy who would be doing the real work. And wasn't it actually quite exciting?

Isaac held the chain up close to Elizabeth's face. Back and forth, back and forth. A crucifixion of sorts.

"Lady Moreton. Elizabeth."

There was a slight murmur at the informality of this address. Sir David glared but Isaac did not notice. He had no thought for anyone else now. He was centre stage.

Elizabeth obeyed the command and looked at Isaac.

"Elizabeth. You must free your mind from the confines of your body, let it drift outside yourself. Break the chains that bind you." This had been his mantra at the start of every performance, every hypnosis. Except that it had always been Lucy's name he mentioned.

He could see Elizabeth's disappearance beginning. Part of her had gone already. Just a little piece remained, bearing witness, trying to fight back. That would soon be gone too.

"Elizabeth. Tell us what is wrong with this boy."

He knew she could not resist.

"I have her," said Lucy. *"We are walking together, hand-in-hand."*

Elizabeth would not be able to not resist Lucy's grip, prevent herself from being dragged into a darkness never experienced before. He kept faith that Lucy would keep her calm.

"Hush," whispered Lucy to Elizabeth. *"You are safe. Remember Isaac has promised no harm will come to you. He has directed you, us, into this child's body. We are here to help him. Then we can return."*

Isaac watched closely, sensed Elizabeth's trust had returned. She was now relaxed and allowing Lucy to guide her further. Now she had to speak.

"Tell them," whispered Lucy to Elizabeth.

And Elizabeth spoke. But it was not her own voice, it was that of a youth, broken, unsure. "Please sir, I feel as if I'm drowning, there is something flooding my lungs…"

A doctor's mutterings interrupted him.

"Bah, we've already tested him for tuberculosis. One of the first things we did. The man's a charlatan." The doctor's companions muttered in agreement.

A flicker of annoyance passed over Isaac's face.

"Elizabeth. Can you see further?"

"Only a little, there are too many shadows to make out anything clearly. It is dark, the dark has always frightened me."

"Don't be frightened. Lucy is there with you. She is holding your hand. Together you must search beyond these shades. You must leave your body to continue your search."

The audience let out a low gasp. He could see them from the corner of his eye leaning forward, every one focussed on himself and Elizabeth.

Somewhere the clock struck the hour. This was the moment that the anchor holding Elizabeth to her earthly body would break free. Lucy already had her in her grip. She had no choice. He gave her no choice. And still he sensed she trusted him.

"Elizabeth. You know what you must do." He used his words to batter her, break her will. The chain swung. None of this worked, he knew that, but still, showmanship counted for everything. Lucy was in control, she was pulling the girl along with her, taking her somewhere. Where would Genesis take her?

"She is safe. A lovely young thing to add to my collection."

Elizabeth by now had become a stone statue. He swung the chain closer to her. Back and forth, back and forth. It was time.

"Elizabeth!"

She nodded. Lucy smiled and she too bowed her head. The cross continued to swing.

Now.

"On my next command, Elizabeth, your soul will leave your body completely and enter into that of the patient."

Another gasp from the audience. Isaac felt the pride within himself growing, he could not stop now.

The two women bowed their heads in response.

"Elizabeth, leave your body." His voice was tense, urgent, all-powerful.

There was a slight residual resistance. Lucy muttered that Elizabeth was hanging on, refusing to let go completely, clinging to herself, her body. But slowly, so slowly, she loosened her grip, unable to hold on beneath the power of Isaac's words, of Genesis and Lucy. It was too much, too much to resist.

And then she was gone, taken somewhere by Genesis. He allowed Isaac to hear her though. He could hear her crying in the darkness, he could feel her terror, and all the time he kept the chain swinging, back and forth, back and forth.

And still Isaac could not stop. The moment was carrying him on. She was no longer there but he had to continue, he had to make a strong impression on his audience, reinforce, in their minds, the power of his own.

He moved closer to her, knelt down so that they were face-to-face, his eyes boring into hers. He could see the emptiness there even as his own shone bright with triumph.

"Elizabeth! You have performed well this evening. Now I have only one more instruction for you. And you must obey me. I order you, I command you, to allow your soul to abandon your body, vacate your earthly shell! Elizabeth—LEAVE!"

He watched as Elizabeth collapsed, a silent moment that felt as if it lasted an eternity. And all the time Lucy just sat there, and it was her turn to look triumphant.

"Consequences," said Genesis. *"You have not thought of the consequences. What will happen now?"*

His words jolted Isaac back to the moment.

We can bring her back, he said.

"We?" Genesis laughed. *"This was all about you and what you were capable of. Besides, it is some time since I added a young woman of her beauty to my collection. I think I will keep her. You will have to deal with... this. Come now. You are my man after all. Show the world what you really are."*

Isaac looked down at Elizabeth, her body prone on the floor, no sign of life. Members of the audience had rushed forward, some trying to revive her. And he knew they would not be successful.

This was what darkness was truly like.

Chapter Sixteen

The voices in his head were all shouting at him. He could hear nothing through the confusion.

Elizabeth was lying in front of him but her eyes were staring glassily ahead. The rest of the company had got up and were starting to crowd round her. The doctor who had earlier challenged his performance was holding her wrist, taking her pulse. He looked up at Sir Michael and shook his head sadly before passing his hand over her face to close those white, staring eyes from view. Then both men looked at Isaac. Moved towards him.

Some of the women screamed.

There were cries of "Murder!"

No, it wasn't possible! Genesis had promised him to give him a gift tonight, he would allow him to separate soul from body. Had he been successful? So far, he only saw a body which everyone insisted was dead, that he was a murderer. But her soul, where had that gone? Genesis had broken his promise.

"No. I promised to help you with the separation. I said nothing about what would happen after."

Isaac tried to push forward but strong arms restrained him.

"You are going nowhere near my daughter," said Sir Michael. "You will remain here until the police arrive."

"She isn't dead," murmured Isaac, "she cannot be. It is a mere separation of soul from body. I *can* reunite them, I *will*. I merely need to listen, she will speak to me, she must."

"Like all those voices you claim to hear from the great beyond in your little shows for the desperate and the gullible," sneered Sir David.

Shocked faces filled with disbelief and contempt stared in his direction, a murmur of outrage slowly growing but beneath it all a feeling, an undeniable feeling, of excitement. And it made Isaac believe he still had them.

He could turn this round, have them eating out of his hand once more. Now the contempt was on his side as he looked round at his audience; their lives were so boring, so empty. They delighted in scandal provided it did not affect them personally, only had them as witness. They wanted something to relieve the monotony of their dull lives; well, he would give them what they asked for.

"Elizabeth," he cried. "Elizabeth, talk to me from whatever realm you are inhabiting, talk to me. I am listening!"

"The man's mad," muttered a voice nearby.

"Should be locked up. The police. Where's the police?" shrieked another.

He fought back their condemnation, closed his eyes and listened to the darkness. She would come soon. He knew she would.

She had to. Then he heard her voice. Inside himself amongst the others. She was speaking to him.

He started to smile and laugh, his expression growing wild in the delight he felt at hearing her speak again. Those nearest to him fell back at the signs of madness that seemed to be taking over the doctor.

"She's not dead," Isaac shouted triumphantly. "I can hear her. She's talking to me, she's talking to me. Do you want to hear what she's saying?"

The arms that held him started to pull him out of the room. He heard a woman sobbing nearby. Why was she weeping? There was no cause for that. No one had died. Why would they not believe him? He tried to get nearer to Elizabeth's body, fought against those who struggled to contain him. More weeping.

Damn these women, Isaac thought furiously, *emotional creatures, no understanding of science, of its purity, of its possibilities*. If only they'd give him room to work. He tried again but more arms claimed him, someone was tying his hands.

"Get that mad man away from here, take him to the study," roared Sir Michael. "Lock him in there… and guard the door."

"But don't you understand," he continued to call. "She's speaking to me, she's not dead, she's not dead, she's…"

The door slammed shut on him and he was alone. And for a moment there was peace, blessed peace; even the voices were quiet.

A solitary lamp lit the study, the fire already dying in the hearth. The light it cast made shadows creep along the wall, dance their way towards Isaac as if to embrace him into their world. His mouth felt dry and clammy. He desperately needed a drink.

He sank into the chair by the hearth. Allowed himself to recall what had just happened. It was Lucy who was guiding Elizabeth. She had promised no harm would come to the girl.

"And it didn't."

He could hear Lucy's voice but she was not in the room. He had been locked in here on his own, like a common prisoner.

"She's safe. You heard her voice."

Isaac closed his eyes, trying to cut out Lucy so he could turn himself inwards, try and find her amongst the crowd that gathered behind his eyes. There was a murmuring there, but she did not respond to his silent calls. Women could be emotional creatures, he decided. She was probably just sulking. Even so…

What was it he wanted? Oh yes, a drink. He turned away from the shadows, noticing a whisky decanter at his side. He slipped the inexpertly tied bindings from his wrists, poured himself a glass. He was still a guest, after all.

He had wanted to possess Elizabeth but not in this way. It served no purpose.

"No?" murmured Genesis. *"You wanted to achieve this separation of entities. You wanted your name known. I have given you everything you desired."*

The door opened and Genesis faded once more.

"Mr Bercow." The man pointedly did not use the title Isaac had given himself earlier. He came closer and Isaac recognised Doctor Havers.

"I have come to make an initial assessment of you at Sir Michael's request. Sometimes the police add more confusion than clarity and Sir Michael wishes to know exactly what happened. As do I."

"Doctor Havers, so nice of you to concern yourself in my affairs."

"What else could I do when I find out that I too have been duped into promulgating this fraud?" Doctor Havers stared angrily at him. "It does not matter what stories you come out with now; they will be given no credence. But I *do* care about my professional status, and I intend to redeem myself in that. You never did attend St. Andrews, did you?"

"Oh, I was there, Doctor Havers, but not so's you'd notice."

Isaac had been there. Delivering bodies, bringing the deaths that Havers required to demonstrate his surgical techniques, his anatomy lessons. Without Bercow there would've been no such lectures.

But when he delivered the bodies in the cart, when on occasion he would push the gurneys into the lecture hall, Havers and the other doctors had always taken great pains to ignore the men who delivered them. They offended their sensibilities even if at the same time, they were providing the surgeons with a vital tool.

Isaac had no such delicacy about him. Dead or alive, a body was a body to him. They evoked no emotion. Love, sorrow, regret, all were weaknesses of the human condition, and he had banished those weaknesses from his life many years ago.

Doctor Havers nodded. "I must ask you about your consultations with Lady Moreton. I understand you used hypnosis on her?"

"I will not deny it," said Isaac. "You, yourself have experienced its efficacy."

"That was a mere aberration," said Havers with annoyance. "I have a strong constitution, one which can fight back from the tricks of the charlatan. It did not take me long to realise what had been done to me. Your little parlour game soon wore off. And as for those threats of violence… well, you will be safely locked up soon, so I have nothing to fear anymore."

Locked up? His surprise amused Havers, who was enjoying having the upper hand after his recent humiliation.

"You claim to separate soul from body. You claim Elizabeth resides in your head. These are fantastic claims, impossible claims, the ravings of a mad man. Where do you think you will go if not the asylum?"

Isaac closed his eyes. Would any of his monsters come forward, speak to him? Advise him? All was silent.

Havers was looking at him keenly. "So silent, Bercow? I have never heard of you being at a loss for words."

Isaac drained his glass and poured another one. He made no attempt to offer Havers a drink.

"Ah, the demon drink," said Havers. "Alcohol is the root of many an evil. What else do you take, I wonder."

Havers just sat and smiled at him. Satisfied that he had diagnosed Isaac as an alcoholic and a madman.

"You wanted to know what I did to Lady Moreton," said Isaac with a sneer. "Are you sure you want to listen?"

Doctor Havers had paled but he steadied himself. What was he imagining? Did he imagine Isaac had seduced the wretched girl? Would it make any difference if he did?

A hint of scandal, perhaps a pregnancy; he would not go to the courts then. No, they would pack him off to the remotest asylum. And such places would not be able to hold him. It was the beginning of a plan, an idea. Backed into a corner, he was coming out fighting.

"So, Mr Bercow, exactly what went on?"

And Isaac told him. Described where he had kissed her, how she had delighted in his caresses, how she had enjoyed herself as well as any prostitute...

Isaac found himself pushed back into his chair. A hand around his throat; perhaps he had been a bit *too* fanciful.

"Tell Sir Michael what you will," he said in the end. "But believe me. Any autopsy will reveal the truth of my statements."

The mention of an autopsy made Doctor Havers frown. It would not do for such an examination to be made. It would be positively indecent.

And so Isaac knew they would not discover that lie.

"And tonight?"

"She was merely acting a part. She was under no hypnosis. It was a trick. I have turned her into quite an actress."

"So, you are saying her collapse was completely unexpected and nothing to do with you."

Isaac smiled. "No, nothing."

"And what of those voices you claimed to hear? You said she was in your head."

"That was but shock, dear Doctor. You must realise that someone very dear to me had just collapsed in front of my eyes. I was overcome."

There were footsteps outside. Sir Michael entered. Doctor Havers immediately rose and took him back outside, leaving Isaac on his own once more.

"Very clever," said Genesis. *"The rat in the trap is breaking free."*

"You do not have any voices you wish to speak to me, to take control of my body, drive me on to some perverse action?" asked Isaac.

"Voices? No, I thought to give you space tonight. To free you enough to be yourself. I have even taken Elizabeth."

Taken? Perhaps they were never there in the first place. Had Isaac been duped, just as he had tricked his own patients?

"You will never know," said Genesis. *"And still you hear my voice. And you see me."*

Isaac stared at the man, watched as he faded, became a mere apparition, disappeared completely. Isaac poured out another tumbler of whisky. The decanter was nearly empty but he did not feel drunk; there was no warmth inside him. Only a dreadful cold that froze his limbs, made his hands shake.

"Greed and ambition, Isaac," said Genesis. *"That has been your downfall, but I have need of men like you. You are my foot soldiers, taking my chaos and discord out into the world. Turning men upon each other, upon themselves. You are my carrier and I still have a use for you, so no, you will not die yet. There will be no hangman's noose. Your cleverness has cheated the hangman of a victim but I take no offense; you have not cheated me yet."*

Doctor Havers returned. "The police have been here, but we have persuaded them it was merely an unfortunate incident. Her family doctor has informed them of the state of her nerves, that she had an underlying weakness of the heart. He has signed her death certificate and there will be no investigation, no inquest."

So far, so good, thought Isaac. But where was the catch? They couldn't just let him go, and the scene in the drawing room would be discussed in many parlours for some time to come.

"They do however want to speak to you as a matter of course. A constable will be along shortly. Sir Michael has decided you are to explain how overworked you have been recently, how… lack of sleep has caused some hallucinations which resulted in those strange references. I have already made a statement to the effect you are in the middle of a nervous breakdown. It elicited a great deal of sympathy."

"So, she really is dead," said Isaac, more to himself than to Havers.

"Of course," said the doctor. "And it would not harm your case if you made the odd reference to hearing voices in your statement. It would back up my diagnosis. I have already explained you have been committed to Arthuret Asylum."

Isaac stared at him in horror. "That is the other end of the country. It is a heathen, barbarous place…"

"You know of it?" asked Havers carefully.

Oh, he knew of it alright. On the border with Scotland, it was as far from civilisation as you could possibly hope to be. Isaac had been committed as a boy after he had killed for the first time. A vicar had taken pity on him, declared his crime was one of a moment of madness, not of inherent criminality, and had his sentence changed. Isaac had hoped for transportation to Australia, a new land, a new life, but instead he had been sent north.

Now he was to be returned. But he had escaped once before, could do so again.

"The place has changed somewhat since your last… visit."

So he knew.

"There is a new regime; healthy diet, plenty of exercise, the latest treatments to cure or relieve disorders of the brain or the mental faculties."

"And how long am I to stay there?"

"Oh, a mere year or so. It depends on your response to treatment."

"And if I choose not to go?"

"I'm afraid you have no choice in the matter," said Havers. "There is no place for you in London. A certain amount of what occurred this evening can be hushed up but some of it will certainly reach the papers, spread your fame, or rather your notoriety, abroad. Living in London would be uncomfortable for you."

"So I am to retire to the country," mused Isaac. "Oh well, I dare say the change of air will do me good."

Genesis was laughing somewhere. The evening was certainly affording him some considerable amusement.

And Isaac gave himself up to the good doctor. Meekly allowed himself to be escorted to an anonymous carriage waiting at the back of the house and closed his eyes as the long journey to the north began.

The motion of the carriage was soothing and he was soon asleep. With no more plans and schemes to consider for the time being, he could afford to rest.

"Don't worry, Isaac," said Genesis. *"I am travelling with you. I still have plans for you and I. After all, Arthuret is where we first met, if you did but know it. And you will meet other old friends there."*

Chapter Seventeen

Doctor Rees Llewellyn was once more walking the darkened streets of Whitechapel. He had not seen Isaac for a number of days and had no wish to, although he had an uncomfortable feeling that one day he would not get much choice. Not if he wished to be rid of the monster that now resided in his head and which increasingly controlled his every movement, even in daytime.

"Hey, Doctor!"

A boy's voice. One of Isaac's little spies, he recalled. He continued to walk.

"Doctor!"

The rascal had caught up with him, now stood in his path blocking his way. He could feel his arm rising, ready to sweep this little bit of filth away.

"It's Doctor Bercow!" spluttered the boy before Llewellyn could let his arm drop.

"What do you mean?" he growled.

The boy backed away. This Doctor Llewellyn was not the one he was used to, not the kind doctor who had always had a good word for him when they met, would give him a penny or something to eat.

Llewellyn noticed, softened his features, although his eyes were still hard, harsh. "I'm sorry, boy," he said. "It's been a long day, a lot of patients. You understand. Now tell me of Doctor Bercow."

And Llewellyn listened in shock and dismay as he heard the tale of that evening's fiasco. Yet even as he realised he had lost perhaps the one route to salvation he had, he rejoiced at Bercow's downfall. He patted the boy on the head, handed him a guinea.

"Cor, a guinea?"

Llewellyn smiled. "Get yourself off the streets if you can. Get away from here. Do something with your life."

The boy's eyes sparkled under the light of the streetlamp as he considered the possibilities. Llewellyn knew he would make great plans for himself and then he would buy himself a pint of ale at some tavern and then, well, he would be conned in some manner. A fool and his money were soon parted. But it was nice to have hope, a vision of a different future, even if just for a little while.

"Thanks, Doc," said the boy and vanished off into the night.

So, I am alone, thought Llewellyn. *Bercow will not be able to help me.*

"*No,*" said the voice he hated. "*You are not alone. And with him gone we are free to do as we will.*"

Which meant night after night of walking sordid streets, through filth and muck, amongst squalor and decay. Taking the lives of those unfortunate enough to cross their path.

He could not bear it. When he closed his eyes all he could see was blood, whenever he looked at his patients he would hear their pulse roar within them, imagine a knife carving through their flesh.

Increasingly his tongue tasted copper, food tainted with the flavour of murder. His family wondered why he would rush out, puzzled at the amount of emergencies he had to attend to recently. Requests for him to go on holiday, to take the air or some rejuvenating spa were brusquely ignored.

His monster was becoming bolder, frequenting more populous taverns. Shaming him with his choice of women. He groaned and the sound echoed up the streets. Tonight, he determined, they would keep to the quiet places.

"And what will we do for amusement in these quiet places?" asked the voice.

Think.

"No. Life is too short to waste your time thinking. We still have much to do, you and I."

Llewellyn used whatever strength he had to direct his body towards the Thames. Walking the banks often soothed him and even the docks with their rough and ready workers showed an honesty in toil that was missing in so much of his life.

"Now, now, Doctor. We don't want to be getting too philosophical, do we?" said the voice impatiently.

"I just need a moment, that's all," said Llewellyn. "Couldn't you at least give me that?"

"Very well, Doctor," said the voice. *"Anything for a quiet life. I'll give you time to collect your thoughts a little. Down near Shadwell is a nice little spot. Once you've done, we can go to the Stairs. We'll take the pick of the bunch tonight in celebration."*

"Celebration?"

"Celebration of our new life. The shackles are gone. Bercow is gone. Genesis is gone. We are free!"

Llewellyn's ears pricked up at that. Genesis? Who was Genesis?

"Just another voice that lives in your precious Bercow. Although the man declares him the Devil, believes he is a separate entity that has taken control of him."

"And is he?" Llewellyn could not believe he asked such a question. A few months ago, he would have scoffed at the idea, now, too much had become uncertain, the lines of reality blurred.

"Who knows?" laughed the voice.

Llewellyn continued his way towards the river. The streets familiar, the destitute faces that turned towards him no longer frightening. These parts had become his home and seemed to welcome him. Groups of men would ignore him, or if he caught their interest would soon turn away when he looked at them. What did they see behind his eyes now? Had the invisible monster really become flesh?

Llewellyn thought back to his life in the valleys. It had been a struggle for the miners he tended but there had been little of the misery he saw here. They worked hard, attended chapel, supported their families. Little of the corruption of the city found its way there. He should never have left.

But his sister had been bored, demanded some element of society with which to mix and so he had brought her and his other siblings to London. With their parents dead, he was the head of the household and he had responsibilities.

It was too much. Always at the beck and call of others. Of his family, Isaac, patients, this monster who now inhabited him. Did he have anything left of himself?

By now they had reached the riverbank. He leaned against the railing and breathed in deeply. The air was fresher here. It washed over him, a gentle caress of his cheek, a lover's touch.

"*Perhaps we should go and find a woman now*," chuckled the voice.

Llewellyn refused to answer. There had been no gentleness in his life for a long time. His sister had tried to introduce him to suitable partners but the creature within had held him back. Scorned them as insipid, lacking passion, God-fearing.

"And what is wrong with being God-fearing?" asked Llewellyn.

"*Nothing. Except it's all lies. Lies printed on paper by men who never even lived at the time about which they wrote. All we get is their version of the truth. Whereas, we... we can make our own. There is no authority over us.*"

No authority. He had no authority even over himself. How long could he live this double life? Soon there would be a mistake, they would be discovered, shamed. The only certainty he felt at the moment was that the hangman's noose awaited. And he was tired.

"*You know your trouble, Doctor?*" said his companion. "*You think too much. You should live in the moment. Follow your impulses whatever they may be.*"

Llewellyn looked into the inky waters below. Further down their path he heard the cries of the dock workers, raucous laughter and shouted curses. Honest toil. There was nothing honest about him anymore. He had broken the oath to protect life. He had a parasite within that drained him of the joy he used to experience in the company of others. Sometimes he felt as though he were no more than a walking dead man.

His thoughts were darker than he had ever experienced. And there was no way to let the light back in.

The river lapped gently on the shore. The tide was in. A waterman had just pulled his boat out and was already making his way across. So much that was ordinary, everyday, was beyond his reach now.

"Follow your impulses, you say," said Llewellyn.

"*I dare you*," said the voice. "*Let's see what you can do.*"

Don't think, just act. Impulse was a foreigner to the careful Llewellyn but now, what else was there?

He grabbed the rail and launched himself over. He heard a laugh as he hit the water, realised it was himself enjoying the fact he had committed this act and his monster had been unable to stop him. The water was cold and quickly seeped into his clothing, making him heavier, dragging him down. He went under.

"*No,*" cried the voice. "*No, we have so much more to do, you and I.*"

And the monster began to battle with Llewellyn then, trying to regain control of the limbs that Llewellyn allowed to float uselessly, trying to propel him upwards.

"*You think you are free of me if you drown?*" he roared. "*Do you not know where all go who commit suicide? You will be with me forever.*"

Llewellyn's body was closing down. He could feel the cold, the pressure on his lungs, his blood slowing in his veins. But his mind was startlingly clear.

Wherever he went, his mind, his conscience, would once more be his own; there would be no parasite within. The Devil and his servants would take him, command him, torment him, but it would be his own torment, unshared. He would rather live in that Hell than this one.

Llewellyn opened his mouth and allowed the water to rush in, drowning out the voice in his head.

Down he sank, further and further. His eyes noticed a body, bound and weighted just beneath him. He was not alone. Other unfortunate souls were with him. The voice in his head had become a murmur. Perhaps it hadn't been real, and this had been one long nightmare. No matter. It was best to finish it, one way or the other. He smiled and the monster roared.

The waters above his head closed peacefully, showing no sign of anything ever having entered there. Nobody had seen him jump. When a search was started the next day, the police reported he had last been seen in the company of a young boy. The lad was later found to have had his throat cut.

Chapter Eighteen

The journey was long but not arduous. Day after day of monotony proved a pleasant blanket that smothered and stilled the nervous energy that had been flowing for so long through his veins.

Doctor Havers travelled with him, hoping to witness the psychosis he was certain currently lay latent within, thoroughly enjoying the feeling of power over one who had bullied and belittled him in his own club.

Isaac knew his faint hold on Havers' mind had vanished and the man was now fully alert to any tricks Bercow might choose to attempt on him. Isaac listened for his brothers, listened for their voices, tried to call his monsters but there was no reply. There was nothing looking out from behind his eyes except his own damned soul.

"Why do we not travel by railway?" asked Isaac, as the carriage jolted him hard against its side. At this rate he would be black and blue by the time they arrived at their destination. "The journey would be quicker and you would rid yourself of me that much sooner."

"And give you an audience if you choose to start playing your mind tricks again or, even worse, dupe some poor soul into becoming your puppet? No, this method is quieter, safer… more amenable."

"You regard yourself as immune then from my particular talents?"

"And what talents would those be? A circus trick with spinning watch or perhaps a more theatrical crucifix? Something to trap the gullible or unwary. I must admit I was surprised you succeeded with me but, now I look at it rationally, I was tired, I'd had a few drinks—of course I was susceptible. I can allow myself to accept that." Havers smiled and turned his face to the window.

"But I notice you never hold my gaze for long," said Bercow. "So you must still fear me, even if just a little."

Havers looked at him. Held his gaze long and hard. It was Isaac who turned away first this time.

The carriage continued to jolt its way across the unforgiving landscape, the earlier ease with which the wheels had flown across the surface long since left behind. Overcast moors surrounded them, skies heavy with the threat of rain; it suited Isaac's mood. He had fallen so far, so fast, an incomprehensible descent in view of all that Genesis had promised him.

Genesis. When would he hear that creature's voice again?

Eventually, they neared Glengarnock and the carriage turned away from the main route. The asylum was isolated; the Board of Overseers preferred to house the insane well away from any normal dwellings. Escapes were rare but they preferred to keep the taint of madness away from the rest of humanity.

Now the carriage slowed as it started that last upward climb. A rambling track, poorly maintained, the loose stones causing their driver no small difficulty.

They could hear his shouts and curses, the crack of the whip and the protest of both vehicle and beast alike. At one point it looked as though they would have to get out and walk for a while as the wheels churned in the cloying mud. Isaac would've enjoyed that, a chance to stretch his legs beneath an open sky. The thought, however. did not appeal to Havers.

"You prefer the filth of the cities," sneered Isaac, annoyed at his continued failure to provoke the man. "Where is the honesty in that?"

Havers ignored him and refused to move, but at that point the driver got his horses going again. Now the asylum loomed over them, majestic in its isolation, a grim and forbidding presence that appeared to offer no warm welcome to any who should come upon it. The dreary walls rose smooth and high, unrelieved by windows or ornamentation, a blank, faceless monster waiting to devour any who would choose to visit.

Despite the years that had passed, Isaac remembered it perfectly. Nor had it shrunk over time as the man replaced the boy; if anything it had grown larger. Grimy gates swung open and the carriage was admitted to the dismal courtyard.

And as Isaac finally set foot on solid ground, he felt his world shift. He stretched out an arm to prevent himself falling but the wagon had moved off. Havers, who stood nearby, made no move to help him. Instead, he stood over Bercow's figure, a satisfied smile on his face. Isaac knew this was where Havers thought he belonged, crawling in the dirt at his feet.

"Don't you have a university to get back to?" Isaac snarled as he struggled back into an upright position.

"Oh, they've allowed me a few days to make a study of you. I will be overseeing your initial treatment, together with Doctor Caul."

This time when Isaac fell, the world went black around him.

When he came to, Isaac found himself in a small room, not quite the cell of his childhood but not far off. He lay there quietly for a moment, surveying the dank, unadorned walls, their cold unforgiving stone holding him hostage from the outside world.

His limbs ached from both the cold and his fall. Raising his left arm revealed livid bruises, a pattern he was sure would be repeated on the other arm, but when he tried to examine himself he felt the pull of cold iron, the heaviness of the shackle around his wrist.

Slowly, gingerly, he sat up and swung his body round. His boots had been removed and he was barefoot. A thin carpet of straw did little to cushion his feet from the cold. In the corner was a bucket which his chain just allowed him to reach. The solidity of the walls was unbroken, except for the barred door.

With effort, he stood up, still swaying slightly, the dizziness experienced earlier not completely gone, and staggered over. Through the bars he could see a dimly lit corridor furnished with a number of other cells much like his own. They appeared to be empty, but it was night and there was little to illuminate what may or may not have been hiding in the shadows within.

At the furthest end he could see a chair, unoccupied. Was the night guard on his rounds already?

He shivered at the thought. That too was a long-buried memory. He listened for sounds of life but there was nothing apart from an occasional rustling in the straw, a flash of something and then gone.

He returned to his bed and closed his eyes against the misery. Sleep would be his escape for at least a little while. Yet it turned out that this was not to be. No sooner had the world receded than he found himself forcibly dragged back.

The door crashed open and unseen figures hoisted him up by his arms; from their strength he gathered these were the men who dragged him into his cell earlier. The chain was released from the bed but the shackles were not removed from his wrist.

Along unlit corridors he was marched, a warren of tunnels, empty and abandoned, until they reached a staircase. This took them up, up and out of the bowels of the asylum to that little part of it which made a pretence at civilisation.

The room was a mirror image of his own study in Waverly Road.

"I wanted you to feel at home," said Genesis Caul.

"I appreciate your consideration," said Isaac, deciding to project a confidence he did not feel.

Genesis walked over to a little cabinet, pulled out the decanter containing the emerald liquid. He raised his eyebrows in question. Isaac could not refuse.

His escorts pushed him down into a chair by the hearth. The fire burned brightly but he felt no warmth. The guards removed his shackles.

"I must apologise for those restraints. Purely for appearances sake, you understand."

Isaac nodded as he took the offered glass. He promised himself he would drink slowly, savour the moment, but when it came to it, he could not help himself. He drank swiftly and deeply. His glass was immediately refilled.

"So now *you* are a doctor?" he asked.

"I am many things," laughed Genesis. "I am both doctor and reaper, deliverer and collector. I am what is needed depending upon the occasion. You must forgive my subterfuge."

"Well, I must confess, I certainly did not expect to find you here."

"I decided a change of scene was due. Sometimes you can have too much of a good thing. I like to move from place to place. And I thought it would be nice to have old friends with me."

Old friends. Who else had he invited?

"Look around you," said Genesis.

And Isaac looked. There was Lucy on her stool, Dominic, Susanna, Mary. There were the victims of those late-night walks of his, Elizabeth, the women murdered by Llewellyn, Llewellyn…

Llewellyn?

"I did not want you to be lonely," said Caul. "They are good company although their topics of conversation are somewhat limited. I will leave you together to get reacquainted."

Genesis left the room. And the voices started again; an accusing babble that grew in its anger. He felt Llewellyn's fury, Dominic's anger, the betrayal of Susanna and Mary. A choir of fear and pain, loathing and hatred, pounded his senses whilst ethereal images floated in front of him and he saw the violence that had been done to what once had been flesh, all on his orders.

He had wanted to know what the limits on morality were, how far you push a person to commit an act so foreign, so far beyond their understanding of what was right, and now he knew. He had proved it didn't matter whether you be man, woman, or child; all were capable of cruelties beyond the imagination once the veneer of civilisation was stripped away. Promise a man money, power, or preferably both, and he was yours, your creature. As he had become Caul's.

The door opened again and Genesis returned with Doctor Havers.

"I'm so glad Havers could join us," said Genesis to Isaac. "I look forward to his observations and assessment of you."

Isaac ignored Havers, tried to speak to his old friends, explain how it hadn't been his fault, how it had all been Caul but still they screamed their abuse at him, crowding in on him so that he had to shrink back in his chair, cower beneath the weight of their presence.

He could hear Havers muttering in the background, giving Caul some trumped-up diagnosis. He struggled to pull himself together, closed his eyes against his assailants but he could not close his ears.

"His behaviour tells us everything," said Havers. "I doubt there is anything more I could learn from observing him for very much longer. He talks to people who aren't there, claims their voices are in his head, has delusions that endanger not only himself but those around him. He is a classic example of *dementia praecox*. It would be most unwise to readmit him back into society."

Isaac realised then how dangerous Havers had become. How much contact had Havers had with Caul previously? Was it even possible that perhaps he had been one of those obscured faces on that evening when Lucy had given her first demonstration? He could not be sure. Except... did Caul have a plan for this doctor too?

Genesis smiled at Isaac. "Why do you always think I have a plan?"

"Did he show these symptoms as a child?" interrupted Havers, ignoring the fact that Genesis had responded to an unspoken question.

Isaac started. Had he met Genesis on his first incarceration here? That was not possible. He would have remembered the man, the face. He focussed on Genesis and it was at that moment that he realised he had never actually seen him, despite the man appearing right in front of him.

Oh, he looked human. Solidly built, tall, well dressed. But when Isaac looked closer, he saw that the flesh rippled as if something crawled beneath, and when he stared at his face, his features shifted and danced in front of him so that he had no way of describing exactly how he looked.

All Isaac could see were Caul's eyes, those deep, dark pits of night that drew him in and showed him his desires, showed how reasonable they were, how Caul could help. And now he realised that he had been nothing more than Caul's plaything, a toy through which Caul could demonstrate his power before he tired of it like any fractious child and cast it off.

Isaac knew that moment was coming for him now and there was nothing he could do. Slowly his mind returned to the study, took in what Havers was saying.

"He was a disturbed youth. Only to be expected when you discover the violence of the father. I am sure you have read his history by now. Unfortunately, the boy somehow managed to escape. I hadn't realised how much information he absorbed from those around him. How easily he could copy our practices.

"He had studied the techniques used by one of our doctors, a Samuel Groves, who had a particular specialism in the field of hypnotherapy. He turned the man's tools against him, managed to escape. Poor Doctor Groves unfortunately died before we could get to him. Isaac had managed to persuade him to hang himself."

That was a lie. That was not how Isaac remembered it. He had spent a small amount of time here, that was true, but Samuel Groves belonged to London, to his days on the streets there.

"Do not believe this man, this Devil," said Isaac.

"You think *Havers* is the Devil?" asked Caul in some amusement.

Doctor Havers, however, merely looked at Isaac in pity.

"Your delusions will prevent effective treatment. I suggest," he said, turning to Genesis, "we start electrical stimulation of the brain. I noticed you are lucky enough to have an electro-magneto machine."

"Only the latest equipment in my asylum," said Genesis.

"I do like to stay at the forefront of technology. Perhaps we should start with the treatment now; no time like the present they say."

And this was it. Once perhaps he would have resisted, fought against what was being done to him, but the voices had become too much. They screamed and howled, their curses merging, berating him for every miserable step he had ever taken.

In his mind he begged for their silence, but they responded only with wild, hysterical laughter.

Havers had pulled a curtain aside to reveal the ignominious-looking machine.

Isaac moved towards it almost gratefully, allowed Caul to strap him into the chair alongside. Watched smilingly as slowly the hand of Genesis turned the dials up, increasing the power so the machine moved from a gentle hum to a louder, more irritating buzz.

But Isaac didn't care.

As the warmth of the electricity swept through him, it slowly shut out the voices, closed them off as if flipping a switch until at last he had peace, blessed peace.

"Good man," whispered Caul as he powered down the machine, released the smiling Isaac Bercow from his restraints.

Stephanie Ellis

"You have proved a remarkably entertaining and resourceful subject, I must say. And for that I will allow an *undisturbed* retirement within these walls."

Isaac was led back to his cell and lay down, still smiling in the darkness that now gathered to embrace him completely.

About the Author

Stephanie Ellis is a writer of dark fiction and poetry with her work appearing in a variety of magazines and anthologies, some of which has featured in Ellen Datlow's Best of Horror recommended reading longlists and in a Bram Stoker Award-nominated anthology. She is a Rhysling and Elgin Award nominated poet and has co-written poetry collections *Foundlings* (with Bram Stoker Award winner Cindy O'Quinn) and *Lilith Rising* (with Shane Douglas Keene).

A hybrid author, her novels and novellas are a mix of self-published and traditionally published. She has a preference for writing in the gothic, folk horror, historical horror and postapocalyptic subgenres but will happily try something new as seen in her alt history cosy crime, *Twiggy Voo?* In fact, she prefers to be known simply as a storyteller rather than be labelled in any way.

She lives in Wrexham, Wales, with her family, where she spends a lot of time gazing out of the window by her desk watching the rain come down—it rains a lot in Wales. This sort of weather is the perfect excuse to stay indoors and read, her tastes varying from Charles Dickens to Ray Bradbury to Tananarive Due to Keith Rosson. She is also not averse to cosy crime in contrast to the darker side of fiction which she both writes and reads.

Music plays an important part in her life and whilst she is a metal fan, she loves punk ('70s naturally) and pagan folk. Gigs attended have been as varied as Nine Inch Nails, Wardruna and Bruce Springsteen. Much like books, she is prepared to try new artists.

When it is not raining – and she has the energy - she hikes hillsides, forests, and canal paths with her husband, Geraint.

She can be found online at https://www.stephanieellis.org and whilst she is most active on bsky: stephellis.bsky.social, she can also be found on Instagram: stephanieellis7963 and Facebook: stephanie.ellis.353.

<u>Publisher's Logistics:</u>

This work of fiction was formatted using 11-point Times New Roman Font, on 60lb cream stock paper. The page size is 5.06" x 7.81". The margins are industry standard, 0.5" all around, with no inside margin, and 0.65" mirrored gutters with no bleed.
The cover is full color in a glossy finish.
The paperback binding is Ingram Content Group's 'Perfect' style.